Pursuit

A Victorian Entertainment

PROPERTY OF
BEEBE LIBRARY
345 MAIN STREET
WAKEFIELD, MA

Praise for Felice Picano

"Felice Picano is a premier voice in gay letters."—*Malcolm Boyd, Contemporary Authors*

Felice Picano is "a leading light in the gay literary world... his glints of flashing wit and subtle hints of dark decadence transcend clichés."—*Richard Violette, Library Journal*

"The Godfather of Gay Lit."—*Richard Burnett*

"Picano has always drawn his main characters as gay heroes, unashamed and unafraid of who they are and what life has to offer, whether positive or negative. This, ultimately, is the measure of Picano's genius."—*Lambda Literary Book Report*

"Felice Picano's contribution to contemporary gay literature in his own work has been immense. His founding of one of the first gay publishing firms, SeaHorse Press, has fostered a profound growth in the gay literary genre. Over the course of the last several decades, Picano, with members of the pioneering gay literary group, the Violet Quill, is responsible for the most heralded gay literature of the 1980s and 1990s."
— *Richard Canning, Gay Fiction Speaks*

"Picano's destiny has been to lead the way for a generation of gay writers."—*Robert L. Pela, The Advocate*

"Felice Picano is a leader in the modern gay literary movement. Among his works are many novels—both gay and straight—poetry, plays, short stories, memoirs and other non-fiction, and service as a contributor and editor of numerous magazines and books. His active involvement in the development of gay presses and a gay literary movement is widely acknowledged."—*Michael A. Lutes, The Gay and Lesbian Literary Companion*

"It is impossible to overate the influence Felice Picano has exerted over 20th Century Gay fiction. His works have shaped the Post-Stonewall landscape."—*Rainbownet.com*

"[Picano]'s a word machine. Yet he approaches the page with a newcomer's exuberance."—*New York Times*

"Felice Picano occupies that rare constellation of literary talent populated by such stalwarts of queer literature as Christopher Cox, Andrew Holleran, and Edmund White."—*Rain Taxi Review of Books*

"Overall, the mature writing of Felice Picano and fellow ex-Violet Quill member, Edmund White, confirms what has been long suspected: the gay writing that has emerged from America over the last three decades is as consistently brilliant as writing has got."—*George Lear, Purefiction.com*

Advance Praise for *Pursuit: A Victorian Entertainment*

"Part mystery, part coming-of-age tale, *Pursuit* follows a young man in 19th-century Europe as he rises from trash-picking ruffian to sought-after lover and trusted associate of the British aristocracy. Picano writes the past with vividness, authenticity, unexpected twists, and engaging language. You're carried along in his adventures from Covent Garden to the Stage and a male bordello to upper crust clubs, cheering for his hero amid danger at every turn."
—*Jess Wells, author of A Slender Tether*

The Lure

"Explosive…Picano plays out the novel's secrets brilliantly, one deliberate card at a time. Felice Picano is one hell of a writer!"—*Stephen King*

"Felice Picano has taken the psychological thriller as far as it can go."—*Andrew Holleran*

"Exciting and suspenseful. A strong plot with plenty of action. Builds to a solid surprise ending."—*Publishers Weekly*

"With its relentless tensions, solid narrative beat, and rising psychological peril this book is a tour de force of gay writing, is one of the founding books of modern gay fiction, and rightly made Picano's reputation. It's got a twist ending, consistently shocks and keeps you gripped."—*Gscene Magazine*

20th Century Un-limited

"Experience once again the genius of one of the LGBT community's best authors and see for yourself where he leads you. You and the history you know will never be the same." — *Lambda Literary Book Report*

Twelve O'Clock Tales

"Think of Picano as a queer literary renaissance man. He writes plays and screenplays, poetry and memoirs, sex manuals and sexy thrillers, historical novels and—this is his fourth collection—short stories. The first, "Synapse," is a creepily science-fictional account of how an elderly man has come to inhabit a boy's body; the last, "The Perfect Setting," is a masterpiece of detection, wherein an obsessive narrator solves the mystery of a landscape painter's murder. Not a one of the stories is like another, such is Picano's wide-ranging imagination; what they have in common is their power and their polish."—*The Rainbow Times*

By the Author

The Lure

Late in the Season

Looking Glass Lives

Contemporary Gay Romances

Twelve O'Clock Tales

20th Century Un-limited: Two Novellas

Pursuit: A Victorian Entertainment

Visit us at www.boldstrokesbooks.com

Pursuit
A Victorian Entertainment

by
Felice Picano

2021

PURSUIT: A VICTORIAN ENTERTAINMENT
© 2021 BY FELICE PICANO. ALL RIGHTS RESERVED.

ISBN 13: 978-1-63555-870-8

THIS TRADE PAPERBACK ORIGINAL IS PUBLISHED BY
BOLD STROKES BOOKS, INC.
P.O. BOX 249
VALLEY FALLS, NY 12185

FIRST EDITION: MAY 2021

THIS IS A WORK OF FICTION. NAMES, CHARACTERS, PLACES, AND INCIDENTS ARE THE PRODUCT OF THE AUTHOR'S IMAGINATION OR ARE USED FICTITIOUSLY. ANY RESEMBLANCE TO ACTUAL PERSONS, LIVING OR DEAD, BUSINESS ESTABLISHMENTS, EVENTS, OR LOCALES IS ENTIRELY COINCIDENTAL.

THIS BOOK, OR PARTS THEREOF, MAY NOT BE REPRODUCED IN ANY FORM WITHOUT PERMISSION.

CREDITS
EDITORS: JERRY L. WHEELER AND STACIA SEAMAN
PRODUCTION DESIGN: STACIA SEAMAN
COVER DESIGN BY TAMMI SEIDICK

For DAVE ANKERS and CHRIS ELLISON

1. Addison's Letters

To: The Earl of R——
11 Hanover Square
London, England

15 September 188—
R—— Manor, Cumbria

My Lord,

Sir, first allow me to utter my greatest mortification and humiliation at the eventuation of events which could not have possibly been anticipated.

Second, allow me to say how your esteemed son, His Lordship's, nuptials and the great galamawking, country estate celebration that ensued here yesterday, I tremble to write it—yet it is so—provided a most devastating commotion. A very large number of people were present from the towns, villages, and farms nearby who attended the fête, and as it lasted so far into the night, a large proportion of them remained upon the property grounds, sleeping in chairs and divans and upon card tables, as well as in several public and even unused private chambers.

The hoi polloi easily undermined my own and my varied underlings' usual methods of vigilance, and, if I must say so, even contributed to my men's confusion and our misunderstanding for some hours afterward. In short, Lord Reginald's wedding celebration, although the event of the season in these climes, appears to have been a carefully selected "cover," allowing his mother, Her Ladyship's, removal from R—— during the early morning hours without anyone being in the least bit the wiser.

Trithers and Sansom swear up and down they

didn't know a jot of such a scheme, and were overoccupied for at least a week past with the many details of the festivities, and they are loudly bewailing the loss of their beloved mistress. After a mid-morning reckoning of all of the servants present, it is believed that there are two missing along with Her Ladyship. One is an apparently well-bred enough lout by the name of Stevens who has been known in the manor and arrived here several days before the wedding. According to the butler, he is believed to have only recently been in the employ of Baroness Ernestine Baggis-Davies, at Hemphill Court, Yorkshire, and to have been "on loan" this past fortnight.

Neither your butler nor head gardener were able to ascertain precisely in what role Stevens was taken onto the staff, one saying he thought the fellow your own "safety man" to watch the valuables, and the other believing him to have been sent directly by Your Lordship for the express purpose of securing the grounds during the celebrations. No further explanations were provided for this unconscionable breach.

In addition, there is a lady's maid by the name of DeBouef or deBouef gone this day who very well may have been Stevens's confederate in the affair. According to the housekeeper, Mrs. Blange, the lass spoke little enough English, but much Italian and French. But this too may have been all of her art. She is believed to have initially been attached to the kitchen staff a month ago as some kind of underhousekeeper. How she then was raised upstairs to be so near Her Ladyship entails a general household mystification. Lady Isolda Chase, née Bouchard, from a distant neighbourhood, appears to have provided Mlle. DeBoeuf's references, although how she actually introduced herself onto the estate remains further mystification. I must point out that both of these referred ladies are long known to be acquaintances of your own, Sir, and have been at varied times guests here. How they were manipulated or "gotten to" in this matter remains at this time quite indistinct.

Amid so much uncertainty, only to be expected so early in my investigation, I can assert that none of your own horses or coaches, My Lord, were utilised. Apparently, a Berline was witnessed very early ante meridian the day of 12 September by the gardener's clearing-up lad. The youth asserted he was awakened early by bad cramps, his stomach unused to the rich cake of the preceding day. He first heard, and only after saw the four-horse vehicle pass by rapidly, given his restricted vision through the demi-lune of the garden jakes. He avowed that the coach moved fast, and its window blinds were fully in place, so he could see no one within.

When pressed, and I can assure Your Lordship, all in your employ have been pressed hard by myself and your men in this matter, Farnsworthy, your head gardener, at long last sputteringly opined that the lad, named Skaggs, John Donald, was probably embroiled in an "amorous encounter" during this avowed witnessing of the coach's abscondence, and not "taking a shite," as he'd declared to us. That sort of encounter would not have been the *first time*, Farnsworthy noted gloomily, and Skaggs was, he believed, to have been in company with a neighbouring tanner's daughter of the same age.

(I hereby recommend that both young persons be inculcated more closely to Your Lordship's cause by various pressures and stresses, physical and mental, as well as dangled rewards for the future. They might prove most useful later on within and without the manor house.)

Allow me to mention that so commodious a vehicle for only three passengers, two of them female, appears to signify that several pieces of luggage were taken during the removal. Only yourself, Sir, and perhaps some on the staff might asseverate for certain whether or not any estate valuables were pilfered, and thus choose to have extraordinary Charges preferred against All or Any of the Perpetrators. The hostelry that hired out the coach has not been identified. Men have been sent out to identify the sources, but I am already fairly certain it will not be one from any neighbouring shires. Your Lordship is held in such esteem that none would dare.

Needless to say, no note has been left, nor any demands. No, nor any missive whether note, letter, or telegram has been sent to anyone on the grounds. Lord Reginald and his new bride have, of course, already left the estate last evening on their honeymoon and you alone would know if they or anyone at the Chancellery has received anything written from the abductors or any demands connected with your wife's return.

What is evident is that her Abductors' plans appear to be farsighted and cleverly constructed, set into motion with great cunning and with a level of surprising resourcefulness.

Your Lordship will understand my own wish to make amends for this lapse and to ensure their ultimate failure in flight. Toward that end, the local railroad stations have been scavenged, such as they are in this out-of-the-way shire, and riders have already been dispatched with instructions to all towns serving crossings by the Irish Sea, our nearest body of water. They are instructed to enquire discreetly, using prudent amounts of coin there and then also at all of the southern Ports of Our Realm that lead abroad. Any information is to be dispatched by return rider directly to myself. Should all fail here, they are all to cross over themselves to Liverpool, Dublin, Cork, Ostend, Dunkerque, Calais, and Le Havre and again pursue their inquiries.

The greatest difficulty we may face, Sir, is the matter of incognito. Veiled women on the Continent, if that is indeed where they are headed, are more common than not. Furthermore, while images of Her Ladyship have been provided along with descriptions, none—whether illustrated, rotogravure, or photographic of any current vintage—is available for Her Ladyship to aid identification. Worse yet, no portraits of any sort might be located for her certain-to-be-more visible assailants. Only descriptive reports exist of them, and those are flimsy at best.

No local or nearby officer of the law nor county sheriff, however, has been notified or requested to step in, as of this date and time, as per your telegraphed instructions. I await Your Lordship's instructions in that regard. I forebear to point out that Her Ladyship herself, according to everyone on staff who was queried, has no obvious enemies, but that Your Lordship certainly does, and those in some quantity, and that this criminal act may have been perpetrated out of that enmity. Aware as I am of your low opinion of the staff at Scotland Yard, they may need to be contacted eventually.

Before that, however, and upon receiving any feasible intelligence whatsoever from any quarter, I endeavour to personally undertake My Lady's recovery and return her myself into your hands, Sir. On that you may have my Oath. I remain
> Your most humble and obedient servant,
> Addison Grimmins

❖

"It will take all day to be delivered," Jenkins complained of the letter just handed to him. "I'll need five changes of horses before I get near London. Can't a telegram be sent?"

"Telegrams *have* been sent," Grimmins said, not hiding his usual handsome sneer at his underling. "This letter must be received this evening."

"I'll be daft if I can understand why."

"Your understanding is irrelevant. Have one of those tarts in the manor house put up a wallet of comestibles for your journey and get going."

"Am I to return His Lordship's answer here, then?"

"I will be long gone from this ill-starred place. Remain at the Chancellery until Stubbins or Seraphim gives you orders."

He turned to leave, but the young fellow, one of his favourites, still hadn't moved.

"Are you still here? Are you in need of a whipping?"

Jenkins sprinted off toward the manor kitchen door and the steed already there.

Grimmins surveyed the place briefly while watching all his orders being carried out. The very last of the invited wedding guests were now disembarking from the manor in their carriages, none of them the wiser of what had transpired. All were now greeted by one or another of the higher echelon servants, each giving the false "regrets Her Ladyship is indisposed" speech. *Hear them clatter along. See the prancing horses, Addison. The rurals in their post-wedding finery.*

He remained at enough of a distance from the front portcullis to be unapproachable, yet close enough to make out each of them, fêted all night, put up for the morning, awakened and fed breakfast, and now dressed and ready to go. He had noted his copy of the manor's invitational list with his own personal comments about each. Most of the guests were, at best, unimportant. Certainly, none seemed to know what had actually occurred; old North country gentry, vicars and their families, a few doughty yeomen and their usually larger families, typical of the populace hereabouts.

Last night, at the post-wedding ball, he'd noted only two beauties. They were not nearly exceptional enough to overshow Lord Reginald and his handsome young wife, in part because neither of the two guests seemed sufficiently aware of their looks, or if so, then neither seemed able to afford the ornamentation to give them more brilliance.

Certainly, one of them, Lady Julianne, knew how to flirt. Daughter of a military OBE now retired, she did so all night long, including with Grimmins, whom she had been clever enough to discover was one of the earl's men. She'd had two of her sisters or friends—they all seemed alike compared to her—surround him at one point during the fête and offer him various delicacies from the punch table, then managed to get

• 19 •

them away while she sought "particulars" about his person and life. She had giggled nicely when he told her that "smart Londoners like myself have lasses like yourself for dessert and leave them without a fare-thee-well." She even had the stomach to say, "Ah, but I don't much care how you leave me. So long as you make yourself difficult to forget." She gained herself a kiss and several unnoticed caresses that caused her complexion to become mottled when the next lad came to remind her that it was her name on his dance card.

 The other standout, a youth named Clive Bradshaw, was a typical Cumbrian lad, straw hair and sky-blue eyes, square jaw and sturdy body, clad in dark blue waistcoat and trousers with an ivory shirtfront that he surely had had bespoke for the occasion. He stood among a half dozen lads of his acquaintance and allowed himself to be pulled into the dances by females quite infrequently and only with reluctance. Two inches taller and two stone heavier than Grimmins, he had enough sense that when he was approached alone upon a terrace drinking punch and inhaling the night air, he knew Addison for Someone. "My Lord," he addressed him and cut a half bow, and then he'd smiled beautifully when told to simply call him "Mister Grimmins." His cast-down eyes had risen several times to meet Grimmins's, showing their little kaleidoscope of hues amid the blue, especially when he'd been tempted with "lucrative employment of a not difficult nature" in London. Doubtless he was correct in believing he was his family's future and support, and yet he also wondered aloud if he might communicate with this representative of the earl's in future, by letter, which favour Addison granted.

 Ah! It had all seemed so comfortably commonplace! And when he thought of it, Her Ladyship seemed in no way aware of her future role of abductee, so easy-going and yet semi-regal was she any time he happened to look upon her. Difficult to believe she was not of noble blood herself, so perfectly had she dressed, looked, and behaved all day and night. But then she had some years of practice, didn't she? He knew when he next appeared among his own men in London, many would be curious enough to ask about her. Few if any of the earl's men there had ever laid eyes on Lillian of R——. She and the earl seemed to comfortably lead completely separate lives. At least His Lordship did, with his private but actually public and quite politically chosen mistresses. No one had been surprised when he'd not come north for the nuptials. He had held an earlier, smaller wedding dinner for the couple. This affair had been for his Borough, his People, and for the newspaper columns.

"Happy to see everyone go?" Addison heard behind him and turned to see that he had company. Mrs. Eagles, he believed she was named. The wife of the owner of a large commercial emporium in ——. And also one of the Marchioness's closest friends.

"Not everyone! Mrs. Eagles," he said, with a modified bow. "Not yourself, surely?"

"Yes, I must," she allowed. "A carriage is on its way as we speak. Ah, there it is now, driving up, and surely they will be looking for me and finding naught but my bags."

"It's unfortunate that Her Ladyship is indispos—"

"Yes, but that was to be expected. Lillian is such a private person, and she rather dreaded all the fuss. Living here so quietly away from everyone," she added with her sharp tongue and sharp eyes in a rather nice face, taking the very words out of his mouth. That was disconcerting. Did she know? What did she know?

Today, like last night, Mrs. Eagles was better dressed than everyone but the immediate bridal party, as she'd

• 21 •

been yesterday. But such was to be expected when one had thousands of gowns and furbelows to choose from. An entire emporium of them, in fact.

"I'll convey your greetings," he said, liking her despite it all.

"Do," she said. Grasping him by the elbow, she had him lead her up to the *porte cochère* where Smithers was looking around in undisguised terror while the expensive landau was being laden.

"I present Mrs. Eagles to her driver," Grimmins said in a loud voice to the aged butler and let go of her without waiting for the sigh of relief from the staff, and then he rapidly took himself away.

She waved as she was helped into the carriage.

Once back inside the house within the earl's study, Grimmins called together whoever was left of his men.

"You all know the Sandy Arms Inn outside Brighton town? That is where I shall be later today. All of you get yourselves gone except Hatch here, who will remain to further on all notes, telegrams, and messages. Arrange to meet me there. Get food from any of the kitchen maids you've been topping or trying to top and get going, all you pack!"

There was a general, semi-amused dispersal from the room. Simons ducked back in with his lopsided grin. "Shall you be wanting me overnight, sir?"

"Haven't I had enough of you?" he asked.

"Oh no, sir. Hardly. I mean—"

"Then you ride ahead of me and let me know if anything comes in the way and meet me there at the Sandy Arms. Secure a chamber for the night."

"Shouldn't someone else remain here, sir? In case she returns."

"Her return here is as likely as you escaping the pox in this lifetime!" Grimmins said.

Simons guffawed, then sped away.

When he was quite alone and the front door once more sealed and the servants about their business, Grimmins couldn't help but say aloud, "The bitch! Who ever thought a female would come to cause me so much trouble!"

To: The Earl of R——
11 Hanover Square
London, England

19 September 188—
Maison d'or-Masson
Dunkerkque, France

My Lord,
   Sir, we have made progress in the search for Her L-ship. A very little progress at this time, it is true, but I believe enough to be built upon successfully.
   As you may deign to recall, horsemen were sent out to all of what used to be called the Cinque Portes, and to three others now more generally in use since that glowing past Era of British Commerce. Two of those eight horsemen produced results. Both reported the appearance onboard their respective ferries of a much veiled and shrouded lady of the correct height and approximate figure, accompanied by at least one male and one younger, foreign-born lady servant. One such trio was headed to Calais, another to this very port I am writing from.
   To Dover went I to see for myself, to ask at the Packet Crossing office of the same fellow for a description. This time, however, and even though I was holding a thick wallet in his view all the time we spoke, he altered his description to that of an ancient wench in veils with a cane and two youngish men. I tipped him lightly—why make an enemy? He may be needed later—and then horsed up for Southampton.
   There, alas, I fared less well. The officer in charge was already across the channel. So, was I then to obtain information of a useful nature from the

seller of the ferry fare? Not so. The Captain of said ferry was in port, and after a tankard of porter, he mentioned he was onboard that very packet crossing with the veiled older lady and her taller young man and foreign maid. Also, during that particular crossing, a passenger of some note—an international visitor—went missing. That incident was more upon his mind and his conscience than any such trio as I wished to know of, about which he was vague in the extreme. He then paid for his drink himself and told me the boat's Purser had some conversation with the three, among other passengers, regarding the missing passenger. This entailed the name and general address of the Purser across the channel, which is now in my possession. So, that then is my next mission, to locate this Purser at his lodging and to question him closely.

Your most obedient Servant,
Addison Grimmins

❖

The packet crossing had been the last regular daily one out of Southampton, and given the month and hour, Grimmins's arrival had not been until after night had fallen, and in a tempestuous storm of grizzled rain, accompanied by howling winds and occasional cracks of lightning that did little to illuminate the French harbour town in which he, along with another thirty or forty seasick and storm-drenched souls, had alighted.

With no known confederates making themselves present despite the telegram sent, he allowed himself to be accommodated for the night in one of the shoreline inns which offered a night's lodging and a bowl of suspicious-looking seafood soup. At least he was among a dozen other, mostly females with children, and elderly at the stinking hostel and thus felt led to believe it was the better of several such hovels the French dared call inns.

He was not abed but a half hour and beginning to drift off, when someone had knocked at the door mightily. Believing it to be his man here in Dunkerque at last arrived, he'd opened the door to face an inebriated lout of a tall, young tar from that same packet crossing boat. The boy began making certain rather unclean demands of him that he might have been amused to entertain were he not quite so exhausted by his day's travel. Instead, all the fellow received was a smart knock of a fist upon his forehead, and the door shoved closed in his face before he could fall over.

He half expected to see the fellow's body still across his room's lintel when he exited. But there was no such sight as he passed down the rickety stairs and sat himself at a rickety table for two in that same unclean dining hall, among many of the previous night's populace, at his breakfast. That meal consisted of a questionable-looking hunk of hard-crusted bread without butter or jam and an undersized *tasse* of the local drink, a very strong black coffee.

Before he could exit the place, two rather contrite-looking sailors in the same not quite sanitary uniform of his previous night's visitor placed themselves in his path, their caps in their hands.

"You must pardon our mate, Dennis," one began. Addison immediately assumed that must be the name of his near-visitor of the night before.

"Must I?"

"Yessir. He was not to know you were a genl'man. He believed you so much resembled a mate of his from another boat, a steam packet across the ocean, as to be that very fellow. He meant no harm."

After a minute of such unclear explication as this, Addison said, "Well, I hope my quick response to his unmerited advances didn't prove too smart for him."

"Oh, no sir. 'Twas his feelin's was hurt, mostly."

Addison decided to make this otherwise fruitless exchange produce some utility. "Tell me, lads, do you know where in this village resides your packet line's purser? I'm told one such fellow does reside here in France, among others of our countrymen."

Mollified by his response and even more by his question, they were quick to point out a street nearby where they believed the purser to live.

He betook himself to this Little Britannia within France, a squalid quarter not far from the silted-up old harbour and previous dockside, which was now utterly fallen into desuetude.

Several six-storey-high tenements tottered together here, their top floors extended wooden front beams which he guessed were once used for hauling weights and lading tackle, and which now met high above the sordid little lanes below, blocking out most light, yet not the sooty rain. Here lived those Englishmen who worked the daily boats across the channel as sailors, stevedores, and lower officers who, for one reason or another, could not or chose not to live in their own land. Some, he surmised, had warrants out upon them for debts, others for felonies, and still others were among the lowest sorts who had abandoned their nation through feeling ill-used by it; still others, he presumed, merely wished to be nearest whatever port allowed them to obtain quantities of inexpensive, easily gotten brandy, by which they were enthralled.

Not a pleasant spot, given the general climate, sliming

everything it touched with a scrim of ocean fog, added to the badness of the morning's weather and the unquestionable penury of the borough. There was a near-thought that tickled his mind without coming fully forward, having to do with the sailor Dennis and his quest. Could he have meant Tom? Addison certainly resembled his brother Tom...No! Of a certainty, Tom was drowned at sea off the coast of Malacca a decade or more ago.

At the third doorway of those tumble-down French tenements, he found an unsurprisingly low condition of abode, yet when he inquired after the purser by name, he was directed within to a coal-warmed and weatherproofed apartment containing more furnishings than the few sticks of furniture and a flung-down straw mattress of those neighbours whose ajar doorways he had earlier passed.

The purser, Crittenden, Jas. by nameplate on his door, was entertaining himself by roasting toast smeared with what seemed to be Stilton cheese over the fire, upon which he closely sat, while nearby a chubby lady in a double apron washed an even chubbier baby inside a pewter bowl, all the while singing.

Finding himself no longer at any disadvantage in this contented little household, Addison relied upon what His Lordship had been kind enough in the past to call his "beauty of person and charm" to ingratiate himself. It helped that he unwrapped a fine rasher of fresh bacon, purchased at the inn. This treat added very well upon the toasted cheese bread, and all of the diners save Baby, who smiled upon them like some tiny Asiatic godling, lit into it with gusto. He'd also purchased and carried a tankard of ale, which they tri-vided.

Like many such creatures who have travelled but little from their homestead, the purser's wife, Mrs. Crittenden, recognized Addison's speech as being not unfamiliar, and when he admitted to being city-born, she soon revealed her own origins as having been near Bishopsgate's less sun-soaked sub-lanes. *Mr.* Jas. Crittenden, by contrast, styled himself a North Ender, hailing from far Middleditch, beyond even Bethnal Green.

Soon they were jolly and cosy, and it was then that Addison pounced catlike yet with so light a paw that the others scarcely felt his claws. Could Mr. Crittenden tell him of a particular trio the Captain mentioned?

In moments, he had received as humorously varied a description of that mysterious ferry boat's passenger register as the purser could provide, complete with a mélange of his clever remarks.

"Under most circumstances," the purser began, "there would have been not a word passed between us all. But then occurred the serious matter of the disappearance of the Oriental gentleman."

He was about to expatiate upon that when Addison asked as simply as possible how the three passengers in question appeared to him.

"Not at all suspicious, sir. It is true both ladies were heavily veiled, but such is now the custom for ladies of station in public. Only the fellow spoke. To my surprise," Crittenden said. "He was quality, that one. Not a doubt about it, sir! My distaff, Polly here, has worked downstairs at some public establishments and says that quality may not be denied ever, is how one knows them in a trice to be quality. And so it was with him. He took charge of my investigation as though I were the passenger and he the sub-officer. And he put me at my ease to do so, too."

"How, then, were the ladies disposed?"

"Both sat close together upon a sort of couch-bench in their withdrawing chamber for hire. The younger seemed to have been reading a book, and though I am not learned, I do know it was not written in English. Nor in French, neither. I know enough of that by now living here as I do. The elder lady held some embroidery all the time. I noticed her gloves had little diamonds above each finger and those were sewn open with silver thread, which my missus says is very fine work and not inexpensive. It was an easy crossing, hardly any pitch, and neither lady seemed at all indisposed."

"Did the older lady appear coerced in any way? For example, had the younger woman any weapon, even an embroidery needle, held up against her as they sat?" Addison asked. "No? Did she look like she wished to speak and was stopped from doing do? No? Did she appear drugged or in any way physically impaired?" No, again.

Crittenden did add how he'd "naturally enough, out of sheer curiosity" followed the trio's movements after the party had disembarked, "despite them being but three out of eighty-six other passengers, as they were so distinctively of quality."

That was how he had discovered she and her companions had taken a public wagonette along with ten other passengers away from the quayside, almost immediately after their arrival in France. He even provided the name of the omnibus driver. That earned him a tip at the door of his flat as Addison was leaving.

"Oh, I couldn't sir, this has been so pleasant."

To which Addison had replied, "Buy something for the lad! A toy. Little lads so love toys."

No sooner had he left than he found and accosted that omnibus driver, who was filling another wagonette full.

"I well recall the party, sir. They remained inside the car after all other passengers had disposed themselves, right until we reached our terminus, just within the city's gates, at the main road headed east. With them was a great quantity of luggage. When I asked if they needed further transportation, the gentleman assured me they were awaiting a private coach."

"So, you didn't see in what direction they went?"

"Afraid, not sir," the owner said. "Back to 'arbour with me."

Damn them! Addison thought. *But this does give me much food for thought.* For if that was as told, it meant the Lady's flight was planned in more detail and even beyond England.

To: The Earl of R——
11 Hanover Square
London, England

24 September 188—

My Lord,
 I am come near to Her L-ship's party. I am but one day and a half at the greatest distance from them now, I do believe, Sir. I beg your indulgence to explain how this has come about and why I have certainty that I shall be able to accost them directly before the week is out. Were the ladies alone, it would a far simpler matter. But the co-presence of what I am assured is a large and stalwart male travelling companion signifies other means will have to be utilised in order to reobtain Her Ladyship.
 As Your Lordship has in the past taught me to do, I separate these into three categories and in fact I am only repeating what has been taught me by Your Lordship:
 First, buying off the male companion. For this, I already hold a cash draught of some size against Your Lordship's account in the Brussels Bourse, and although it would pain me to expend it, I would if this fellow is employed merely as an adventurer for pay, I know that you, Sir, are prepared to lay out for such contingency.
 Secondly, subterfuge. Say by gaining the trust of one or another of the two servants—most likely the chambermaid—and by utilising that wedge to drive them all three apart, I could extract Her L-ship from beneath the many eyes of her Cerberus.

Thirdly, force. For obvious reasons, the least amenable choice. Still, it must be fallen back upon should nothing else work. I carry with me appropriate weapons, including a poignard, and one of the new models of American repeating pistol.

How I came so close to them is surely Providential; the Gods do shine down continuously upon Your Lordship's affairs. Gaining the paid trust of certain locals I followed the path of the Three from Dunkerque to...

❖

Lille, a fine and grey stone city, Addison had been told, was the cynosure of Flanders, known worldwide for its wonderful cloth manufactures and pottery works and for great annual fairs at which those wares were displayed and sold to all of Europe and even beyond.

Upon his arrival, it was clear the town had one foot in the past and one in the future. For, hard on the left, within a few yards of the terminus of the stage coach from Armentieres he'd been told to look for, lay the excellent new train station, only a few years old and already quite hectic with use.

He had arrived here through what must, he had to admit, be accounted a fluke. Like his lord, Addison was not as easily admissible to such as accidents or flukes as he preferred careful planning and sheer indomitableness. Even so...

Returned to the French harbour and being forced to consider what road next to take, Addison had placed himself at one of the trestle tables of the inn, where he considered whether or not to post a new letter, knowing he had little new information but that His Lordship wished to know hour by hour what progress he might be making.

He was poised over such a missive, unwritten save for its greeting and date, when he couldn't help but espy a boy of perhaps nine years and of especial dirtiness paused at the nearest other trestle table, staring at him.

"If it is food you want, you are out of luck," Addison said. "The kitchen, such as it is, is shut."

"No, sir, I have ate," he answered. "But I live next door to 'em, and o'erhear you afore wit' the Critterins."

"The Critterdens, mean you? The purser and his wife? Well, what of it?"

"The three you seek!" the boy began. "I knows more of 'em."

"Indeed. How?"

"I unlade the omnibus for tips."

"Do you now? And did you unload their many bags and cases yesterday?"

"Aye! Ten in all by my accounting. And well paid by 'em, as well, with a hunk o' sweet bread from the dark little lady. I waited, didn't I, at her askin' till their new coach came, and then didn't I help lade them baggage up again."

Before the boy could say another word, Addison had leapt up from the table and grasped him by one dirty ear, dragging him over to the omnibus station, where the owner admitted that the boy helped out.

"Now, for another tip, my lad, enough for much more sweet bread, tell me what more you know. And it had better be worth my dirtying my fingers."

"To Armentieres, then. To town's centre plasse 'otel. The genl'man said."

"To whom did he say that? To the new coach driver?"

"Aye. Etienne, his name, the genl'man. The driver did ask first."

"Etienne? You swear that?"

"So was he called by coach driver." The boy put a dirty hand upon his filthy shirtfront in the general direction of his heart in avowal.

"Etienne, then. And headed to the central *place d'Armentiéres?*"

"Aye. So do I swear it as I 'eard it!"

"Is there nearby a *boulangerie*?" And when the boy nodded, Addison followed him to the bread shop where he bought the boy the largest loaf for sale, as well as two egg tarts, which the happy boy gobbled up on the spot. "This *pain gros* is for your mother, yes?" He handed him a handful of *centimes* which he wrapped in a twist of paper that had begun the unwritten letter, and the boy stuffed this deep in a pocket.

Not long after, Addison was mounted and on the road northeast.

At Armentiéres, he stopped at the hotel in the centre of the town, where he was told the coach he sought had indeed stopped. But he was dismayed to learn the travellers had not taken rooms there, but merely refreshed themselves an hour or so before heading out again to Lille. So Addison also changed mounts, drank some wine, ate some bread, and was soon enough on his way to Lille, which he reached by early afternoon.

This time he also went to the central plaza. But there were several hotels and a new train station, too. His natural assumption would be that the three would abandon the outmoded method of overland horse-drawn transport for the newer, faster, and more luxurious mechanical one. But, Addison reminded himself, if the Lady had not been coerced, then she had left of her own accord. Why, he could not guess. They must now be runaways instead of kidnappers and victim, and, in many regards, no better than a Negro slave would have been in the Carolinas before the great American Civil conflict.

So, while he did discover the train went to Brussels and other cities directly, he turned his attention to the stagecoach, which, the helpful *concierge* at one hotel had told him, at certain times of the week provided as commodious grounds for travel as the locomotive, and was preferred by many travellers.

He found the coach's owner, plump and filling his messily moustachioed mouth with hunks of a very ripe and aromatic cheese, ensuring a distance between the two. Since Addison was well and tastefully clothed, carrying a small if not inexpensive *portmanteau*, the owner, a florid Flanders fellow with oddly accented French, was eager to talk. No sooner had he finished off the dairy than he lit into a half peck basket of elderly strawberries, occasionally spewing red juices about his person.

He began by decrying the rival railroad. "'Tis but a passing fad, M'sieur. Accept my word on it. With its great stench and its noise, with its contamination of the very air that we breathe, M'sieur, it cannot last more than a few months longer. Not one of my regular *customes* have taken it more than one time. And they have returned with great tales of mischief and disdain."

"While your own accommodations…?" Addison prodded.

"Ah, M'sieur, Columbert's Stagecoach Deluxe we supply twice weekly, and more often upon request. By itself the carry-age has triple times the support for the car itself, making a ride smooth like that of the flying carpet of Persia! Then, Columbert's Stagecoach Deluxe provides six—not four only but six!—fine, fat, and fast *cheval* and in addee-seeon, a methodically spaced-out change of steeds, at several extremely re-pu-table inns and auberges, all of quality prem-ee-air and so well worth the cost."

When Addison heard that, he whistled in dismay. "Surely that must only be for the affluent."

"But no, M'sieur. I've had them to run three times a

week of late. And not one day past, a trio of distinguished foreign travellers have one Columbert's Stagecoach Deluxe stagecoach hired entirely for themselves."

"Truly?"

"Among the finest of gentry. They have their own basket-meals prepared for them beforehand. That is how useful our service is. That is how eager those not completely mad for steam locomotives are to make use of them."

Even before the garrulous coachman described them, Addison had little doubt who they were. As for their path, that too became clear: Tournai in half a day; across the River Leuze and into the county of Hainault. The town of Mons by nightfall; then Charleroi, Namur, and Liège the second night. Across the great Rhine River by morning, and by three of the afternoon, the third day, arrival at that one-time centre of the Holy Roman Empire, the German town of Aachen.

Addison's small repast was by this time ready, and he excused himself vowing to return and experience for himself this marvel of the age, Columbert's Stagecoach Deluxe. Not long after he had dined, Addison was penning both a note to be telegraphed to his Lord, as well as a longer missive. In the longer one, Addison detailed his conversation, adding, "Shall Your Lordship think me very naughty, or instead very much Your Own Student, if I now reveal that having obtained this detailed information from the meritorious Columbert, I stole away into the steam train terminus, where I have discovered connections to take me to Aachen in half the time required by the Stage? So, without a care for the poor man's decaying trade nor his self-betrayed information, I am about to entrain. This letter will leave the train at a small mail drop. I know that you wish me, Sir, naught but the greatest fortune."

To: The Earl of R——
11 Hanover Square
London, England

27 September 188—

My Lord,
I am an ass, I am a jackanapes; a lower fellow never existed. My damn pride continually gets in my way, and alas, that of Your Lordship.
They were in Aachen. Were in Aachen. Of that little bit of information, I am now, three days later than my last letter to you, certain. But they left after only one other evening and they have gone to—the Devil knows where!
Let me spell it out in order, for I have been disorderly in my pride, thinking I was so close to them, and that was my undoing.
I arrived here by train as I mentioned in my last letter. There are only a half dozen hotels nearby the hotel, and only two of those are manned by those speaking languages other than German.
This was my first mistake. I thought Her Ladyship's Cerberus little but a muscular dolt, certainly not an educated person. In this was I wrong because not one of those two hotels I checked into, one each of my first two nights in this infernally dull town, knew what I was talking about when I asked if my elder British cousin, travelling in veils with a man and chambermaid, had preceded me since we were to meet up here.
No such woman had shown up. All their custom for the past week had been young people, officers of

the Emperor's forces on leave from duty, and a few commercial travellers. At first, I racked my mind. Had they broken up the trio? Had the girl gone off in disguise? Had both women gone in disguise as soldiers? No, it was too mad to contemplate!

I must confess to Your Lordship, I fell into an hour or two of despair, and took myself out to one of the numerous biergartens that litter the vicinity of the terminus, frequented by students and tradesmen. It was at one of those, on my second and gloomiest night in Aachen, that I traded despair for insobriety and insobriety for dissoluteness. They shut their doors early, these biergartens, and although inebriated, I was cast out upon the streets with the other local drinkers.

These all staggered off, I guessed, to their beds, but I would have none of it. Recalling one of your Lordship's own anecdotes, I asked for G— Strasse, and was pointed toward it, not far from where I leant against a wall to make water. When I found the street, it was as wondrously and unseemly populated as Your Lordship had described it. Nor did I need even to step into one of the establishments of questionable repute Your Lordship had mentioned, but found my female entertainment easily enough in the very first doorway.

It was the following morning as I attempted to secrete this young person out of my hotel room that I discovered my guest's bilingualism, for the words of passion are as deep and meaningless as Babel. Thus, my new friend became my cicerone, and for the price of a bread, sausage, and egg breakfast, I suddenly had the fluent German I required.

Thus it was I discovered my elusive trio had lodged at one of the most authentically German of the hostels, the fourth one I visited in her company. The rather stern woman behind the desk who gave my local charmer the information assured us the Lady who'd stopped there was a German Baroness from somewhere in the East—"Prussia or the Sudetenland, given the accent"—while her chambermaid was an Italian contralto fallen on hard times, and her gentleman a "Herr of the highest German education and scruples." This she knew because he gave as a reference a well-known Professor of Philology at Heidelberg University. They indeed stayed but one night and were aimed toward Munchen, but instead received some news or telegram—not through her office, however—which sent them back again westward. The porter heard the man direct the cab driver to the railroad terminus street side for trains to Brussels, Ghent, Paris, and Rotterdam. Having heard their earlier plans east, he sought to correct him, and received only half a tip for his trouble.

And so, Your Lordship will, I am certain, come to the identical, horrid, conclusion I did. They and myself must have been walking in Aachen the very same day. The same hour. Who knows, we may have passed each other on the same street. My blood runs cold thinking of it. Of course, following this new blow, I no longer had any direction to go in pursuing them. But I have taken your always apt advice. When you have no set direction, stop and think. Something will come to you.

Your most humble and obedient servant
Addison Grimmins

❖

Addison was about to savour yet another enormous supper of spiced sausage and potato with gravy and hunks of brown bread to dip it in, when his charmer of the previous night appeared and, easily finding him by the lamplight, sat down at his table.

He'd already made it clear to Nelly he'd not require her services again, and was about to repeat that when she surprised him by asking, "You must very much this elder relation locate?" When he'd nodded, she told him, "To find in this or any city will be difficult." Which he already thought was a foregone conclusion. "I have cousin," she said. "Woman who knows these matters and can help."

Nelly's cousin—if that's who this Wilfriede actually was—seemed at first more poorly clad and twice her age. She had been waiting outside and came in at her cousin's beckoning.

"How can she know anything?" Addison asked.

"She is with her mind at times able to go far away and see as in pictures."

Nelly then repeated that in German to Wilfriede, who asked something Nelly translated as, "Have you some belonging of the ladies?"

Addison had two: one, a lace-edged handkerchief, believed to have belonged to the chambermaid; but more crucially, he had a thick ring of yellow gold left behind by her Ladyship, a gift from his Lord, and which her servants agreed she had worn daily until her disappearance.

Wilfriede took up both items in one gaunt hand with its sticklike fingers and nodded yes. But Nelly said she must have food before she helped and that when she did help, it must be done in some place of quietness, not here in this noisy restaurant.

Addison fed both women, which was inexpensive enough, after which all three stepped out together, toward Wilfriede's home.

Addison almost asked to stop off at his hotel for his pistol. But he had a penknife with him, in case any trouble was afoot. They walked a good fifteen minutes, and he was about to flag down an omnibus when Nelly said they were nearly arrived. Three or four shops fronted a cavernous, doorless foyer which he peered into to see it was a front building, with a paved courtyard and another somewhat larger edifice behind.

"Please, here. She cannot take money, but it is not very often she may have a sweet." Nelly took him aside to one of the shops, a bakery where she had him purchase what she called *apfel strudel*. This was a flat sheet of long fruit pie some two feet in length which was wrapped in a waxy parchment paper for them to carry.

Once inside the back building, they ascended a dark, wide, open metalwork stairway to a fifth or sixth level, yet another place to be cautious, and he was. A battered door led to a narrow chain of rooms, most of them windowless, all with some kind of bedding, but otherwise vacant. Wilfriede, the mystic, could not wait but must take the strudel to yet another room where Addison was certain she nibbled at it immediately.

He looked about and saw that the room, although poorly furnished with a deal table and a few spindly, dowel-legged chairs, was scrupulously clean. Even the few scraps of some worn, patterned carpet protecting their feet from the about to be caved-in wooden floor looked spotless.

In minutes, Wilfriede reappeared and sat herself opposite Addison, and the reading ensued. Once again, she took the handkerchief and held it in one hand and lifted it quite high in the air. *"Fahr die madchen!"* The chambermaid was far away. Then she held the ring tightly in her hand, and shut her eyes, saying, *"Unglucke die Weib,"* which Nell translated as "a very unhappy wife." Addison didn't doubt it by this time, and so let her continue.

He was handed a set of cards, each more than twice the size of his hand, of which Addison could make out only the backs decorated with various symbols. He was told to sit and "clear the mind" as though that were at all possible, and then to manipulate the cards. He was to lift those to his left side until ten cards were removed. Then he was told to remove another seven cards and to place them, again face down, to the right side.

Addison did so, feeling rather foolish, for he felt no affinity for any of the cards and had chosen them more or less haphazardly.

Despite this, when Wilfriede, still wiping off strudel sugar from her lower lip, picked up the first packet of cards, turned them face up, and looked through them, she began murmuring. She cleared the table of all but the second, smaller packet, which she shunted aside.

Upon the tattered linen table covering with its crudely sewn pattern of children's boats, she began to place Addison's chosen cards, face up, speaking all the while. He asked her cousin to translate, and he began to take dictation, so he might later reproduce accurately what Wilfriede told him. If he was not utterly edified, then at least he would have been diverted for the price of their dinner and dessert.

"This card represents you, Seeker," Wilfriede began. "Darkness descended upon your life early, and has risen only occasionally. You are the Knight of Swords. Vengeful and ruthless and unceasing in his quest."

Addison had to admit he was a bit taken back. He had

been nothing but generous and polite to either of these German women. Yet what she said was not in any way inaccurate as to his character or his mission, and so he listened carefully as she dropped her second card. "This card is your Quarry. The Queen of Cups reversed. A woman made for happiness, but it is snatched from her time after time. This card below you shows you have none or a very small acquaintance with the lady."

That was true enough. He'd met her once and seen her twice. "Four Cups reversed—four upheavals of her womanly affection. This card placed above you shows you hunt her for another, not yourself. Wands Ace reversed. A great person seeks her, and this card bodes some success."

How she could have known all that was so far only mildly remarkable. After all, he'd not said more to her cousin beyond that he had a mission, and was thwarted. "Behind the centre," Wilfriede continued, "lie Nine Swords, reversed. Your Quarry feels she had true reason to be as she is." Addison didn't for a moment believe that. Not a single foul word had been said against her so far by anyone he'd spoken to, nor in London, nor at her home. "It is yourself to be a great troubled life, now changed mostly to good. Before you, Eight Wands, travel, direction, but it is reversed, and so it means no easy route but instead setbacks, delays, and detours."

That was disheartening if true.

Four cards remained, and she placed them to one side, going up vertically. "Page of Swords is you, made younger by the newness of your travel. The Emperor is the card of your friends. Very great persons surround you. Next, your hopes and fears, and this is curious. It is High Priestess, which defies direct meaning, saying instead what is hidden will be revealed."

"Hidden about the lady? My relation?" he hastily added.

"Perhaps. But this is more than lady alone. What is hidden long time now will be revealed."

Wilfriede reached into the other pack of cards she'd had Addison set aside and asked him to pick two. He did and turned up the Knight of Pentacles, followed by Five Wands. "This man," Wilfriede said, "opposes you with all his heart. He is like stone." Her Ladyship's Cerberus and guard, she meant. The last card was the end of it all, and it was the Star, reversed, another ambivalent card. "Your wish comes true. But is what you have wished? Truly wished for?"

That was all he needed to hear. He threw another few coins at her and stood up to go.

Wilfriede, however, held his arm with one claw of a hand tightly and she would not let go until she had used the other to lift and peer at the next five cards in her hand.

She looked oddly at Addison and said in a suddenly lowered voice, and in English, "I beg at you, Herr. Do not more this quest after next halt!"

"The next *halt* is Munich," Addison said. "Where does my quarry, as you so nicely put it, go from there? Shuffle your cards and tell me what they say."

"I do not, I cannot! Ah!" She stopped, for a card had fallen out of the deck of its own accord. Before she could fold it back into the deck, Addison had grabbed hold of it.

Die Sonne, it read, and even he knew that much German. "The Sun!" cried Addison. "Where does the sun shine most brightly? In the south. She goes south from Munich! And there shall I follow."

Wilfriede continued holding his arm, her cards fallen to the table and even to the floor, as she cried something, he could only make out as: *"Cicatrich Halb Mond! Halb Mond! Nach ist die Morder."*

But Addison already knew now what he needed to know.

Once out on the street, he found out from her cousin what Wilfriede had cried out as a final warning. He was to be of extra care about someone with a half-moon scar because near that man was murder.

Back in his hotel room, Addison celebrated with brandy and then hot-temperedly bedded his tart of a translator. For he knew where the three of them were headed now, and it made sense: south of Munich lay the Alps, and through the Alpine Brenner Pass lay naught but Italy. What more southerly place to go?

1 October 188—
Hotel Mercurio,
Bolzano, Italy

My Lord,
As you read this, I have arrived in Northern Italy. I waited three days for the little narrow gauge train to arrive in Innsbruck. I'd been forced to wait because of the impertinent weather, which insisted upon storming and snowing, although it is rather still autumn and far too early for suchlike.

That little Austrian town became agog and overcrowded with winter sporting folk. Yes, you read aright. They come from counties all around at news of a large snow-fall, and they strap on to their boots slats of wood with curved-up ends, and they wield poles for balance—I think mostly for show—and then they traverse the four-foot-high snow banks which cover up all the streets and make carriages laughable and only sleighs at all usable. The people here refer to this walking upon snow with wooden poles as schussing, an execrable word, which like much of German actually sounds just like it occurs. And everyone around me for the three days was mad for sledding and rolling about in snow and for skating upon the ice, which last I have done once before in England. Above all, they are mad for this schussing.

And now I am in Italy, refreshed and quite eager for the hunt again.

Your most humble and obedient servant
Addison Grimmins

❖

Worse than the young men were these Alpine young women. They didn't wear skirts, but instead a sort of woollen piece, both blouse and trouser, that closely covered their bodies from within their boots all the way up to the top of their head, where it was finished off with a little hooded beak, like a bird's, but flattened out. This latter, Addison had been told, was necessary to keep out the sun, since in the mountains it often would become very sunny and so hinder one's vision due to all the reflection from the snow. Needless to add, wearing these *schuss* costumes, the young women looked much like the young men, except naturally for assorted protuberances, which in fact made them all look highly improper. Not that Addison had any complaint.

The scene of these odd activities was the slopes outside on several sides, slopes being the term used for the angled sides of the higher hills and mountains covered thickly with snow, for the people climbed as high as they possibly could up the mountains and then, for fun, they *schussed* down as far as into the town's streets and squares, which everyone else seemed to accept in good humour.

Addison had time for all of these contemplations and speculations since two sudden and enormous snowfalls had left him twiddling his thumbs at his inn with no more entertainment than very old issues of English periodicals—*Longman's Magazine* and *The Fortnightly Reviews*, one with a strange tale by Wilkie Collins and another, even more eerie one, by Amelia B. Edwards—as well as a half dozen issues of *Boys of England* magazine and a battered and somewhat dog-chewed copy of *Robinson Crusoe*, all suggesting some of his younger countrymen had been installed in these quarters not long before and probably also snowed in.

On the third day of heavy snowfall overnight with no

transportation out of town but sleighs and those only locally, Addison felt he had to escape this chalet or he might go mad. So, he decided to step outside and himself *schuss*.

Being still young, in fine physical form and still rather limber, he allowed himself to be led by the trilingual adolescent son of the innkeeper to a dressing room and there equipped with one of the *schuss* overall coverings.

"No! No! All the clothing must off go!" the lad commanded, laughing.

"Not this too?" Addison said, clad only in loose cotton underpants.

"And why not?" he said, pulling his own suit open to reveal a puff of blond hair and genitals.

Addison realized at that moment precisely how British he was, and while it was only in the past several years he'd actually come to don under-briefs within trousers, he now felt them incumbent upon his rank and station, dubious as those might be.

"Also these." Wolfie thrust a pair of long wooden slats with upcurving fronts at him which Addison recognized would become his only, fragile if not actually perilous, vehicle this day. Some thin, pointed ash wood canes were tossed at him, and together with Wolfie's brother, Anton, and another friend, all of them leapt up into an open wagonette headed for the edge of the town.

Several other Germans, an Austrian, and a Swiss couple were already *schussing* down the treacherous incline, as their one-horsed wagonette trudged up a tortuous path. Once arrived and alone on the little plateau, the lads showed Addison how to handle the canes, imitating the side-to-side movements needed for the actual *skees*, as the slats were termed.

The two other boys then took off down the slope and

could be heard calling out to each other. Their heads, then their speeding figures, then only their shadows were visible and they *schussed* away.

"I must be completely mad to attempt this."

"You are a good-looking fellow," Wolfie said. "I am certain you have much experience with the womens. This is not so different," and he slowly moved his hips side to side in a semi-circular motion as though in the throes of physical passion, exaggerating the motions. "You see? You already know how it is done."

Addison did see, and so he let Wolfie give him a little shove from behind. He clutched his canes and he swayed side to side and soon he was moving, sliding along the snow with a mere touch of the ground with the one hand-held cane for better balance and then another, and he was off.

He heard Wolfie pass by him, going much faster. Soon, Addison was all alone on the slope, moving rapidly, never completely stable or secure, with the *skees* below him having some sort of life and mind of their own. They needed more guidance of a hip or arm, but not too much, merely a light touch or motion, and he found himself drinking in the sharp, odourless Alpine air, and having time to look beyond himself at the mountainous scenery as it turned slowly, almost majestically about him while he continued to descend.

Suddenly he heard the voices of others on each side of him. He panicked for a second, but they were past him so rapidly he was able to regain control, until he saw ahead an open landing where Wolfie and his brother and friend were stopped, chatting and looking at him.

"How do I stop?" he called out, but Wolfie just looked startled, then took a few steps forward and called out to someone behind him in German phrases he couldn't make out.

All at once, Addison was in the midst of three others *schussing* closely.

One on each side held him by the elbow and they all landed together just beyond Wolfie and his group, upright for only a moment and then down and all together, him and one lad on one side and a lassie on the other side and two more behind him, all grunting as they fell mixed up in a pile of limbs not far from the edge of someone's storage barn. They laughed and tried to get up, pushing each other down as they did, then throwing snow at each other with no respect for sex, until they were all laughed out.

"You have been so brave and you have now *schussed*, English fellow!" Wolfie said, tapping his chest. "Come, now we go again." And before he could even get his balance, Addison was being lifted into a horse-drawn sleigh for six, and they headed for a somewhat higher slope. This second time, Addison managed to stay completely on his slats, or *skees*, as they called them—and then he joined them in falling atumble at the ending, laughing and pushing each other down again.

"What you are saying?" Wolfie asked.

"This tomfoolery is just…"

"Wonderful, no? Full of the wonder?"

"Yes, wonderful," Addison admitted to Wolfie and the others, laughingly repeating it, and then to himself, last, thinking *not since I was a little child and tumbling about on the dirt floor at Villas Sheen with my brothers…* But thinking of that could only lead to the darkest of thoughts.

Felice Picano

5 October 188—
Casa Ippolito Nuovo,
Ancona, Italy

My Lord,

    Not knowing how long I shall be here, I have taken chambers. They are above a shop that sells baked goods and so I am next door to a bakery, awakened by the aromas of fresh-baked bread and sent to sleep with the perfumes of sweet cakes. Doubtless if I remain long, I shall grow quite rotund.

    I had hoped that with the train delayed so long in Innsbruck, I would encounter Her L-ship or the maid or that lout in the town, or even upon the little train. I could sense Her or at least Someone, the way you have narrated to me you instinctively "feel that your prey has arrived" when you ride out with a gun and hounds into your forest seeking game.

    I scoured the train top to bottom in as normal a fashion as I could, which is to say, curiously but without seeming to be looking for anyone in particular. I encountered enough oddities: a pair of young Greek lads, possibly students, who attempted to engage me in conversation in Italian, and then in very poor English. They are in Italy, but they don't know how long. One was excessively pretty and well worth a tumble. They weren't absolutely travelling alone as I'd at first presumed.

    Coming back through the cars, I saw them with a tall fellow with mutton chop whiskers, whom I'd briefly seen in the wintry Austrian townlet I wrote of to your Lordship. I'd hardly remarked him there. Here, he seemed another traveller. Is he German? He barked a greeting at me in that language. Even later, I saw the Greek students talking to a pert little wisp of a thing who looked at me a long time with very large dark eyes. Now there's someone to tumble, albeit I already know what she has to teach.

Yes, it's boring to talk of potential conquests. But I am bored. I go about the town, and I look for clues to where Her Ladyship may have gone. None have come my way, and I am reminded by the keeper of this house that many leave off the train and remain at Lake Garda. Should I track back and go there? Tourist spots are so boring. They must come through here to get further south, to entrain to any of the larger cities of the Italian Peninsula. Of that I'm certain. And so I shall remain here and rather thoroughly bore myself. Unless, that is, I find something to do.

Yr Obt Srvt,
Addison Grimmins

❖

The days did drag on, despite the mostly sunny weather and lack of anything more than the slightest chill in the air. He easily made friends with Signora Faschiletti, the landlady of the *Pensione Ercoli*, and with her landlady friends from nearby pensions who all met in her breakfast and dining room to play cards daily, after the one p.m. bells had been rung by one of four nearby churches. They played for hours sometimes. One game he'd never seen played before, they called baskets. Another seemed not unlike whist but was played by four at minimum. There were little piles of metallic buttons—painted gold, silver, bronze, and a bluish tint, perhaps pewter, perhaps lead—by each of their cards, which they tossed into a centre "pot," so they might actually be gambling, though he never saw any money pass hands.

One elderly, well-put-together man attended. Nattily dressed and never without spotless spats on his polished boots and an ivory-tipped, turned wood walking stick, which he leant on while slowly ambulating, he arrived and left the stick prominent upon a chair by the doorway along with his grey suede gloves and dove-grey fedora. He was quite distinguished looking with his cloud of cotton white hair and a Roman visage only spoiled by an extended and rather purple lower lip. This Signor Marcellini sometimes played, but more often merely sat and watched while gulping down what seemed the maximum number possible of a local *apertif* called Limoncello these women put up themselves.

He never once directly looked at Addison, not even when they'd been introduced, which he noted was often a sign that a man was physically attracted to him. So, naturally, Addison asked about him to one of the housemaids who were constantly bustling about the third-floor corridors on one errand or another. She insisted the *Avvocato Marcellini* was a bachelor and was believed to have been a noted ladies' man who had unquestionably bedded all of these women and perhaps scores more, and might still be doing it, passing *billets-doux* under the enamelled card table for assignations.

Addison sat in on a few hands, but one game looked a bit too much given to chance and the other too complex for him to bother to learn it with the intention of cleaning them out. But the Signora F. one morning said to him, "Do you think the *Avvocato* is a confederate of ———," naming one woman who had been rather on a winning streak. He replied perhaps so. Then he asked did the Signora F. herself want a confederate at the table? He already knew they called him *Il Bello Inglese*. Each of them found her own way to flirt demurely whenever he'd show up or tip his cap to them. One insisted he imbibe a tiny, bitter cup of coffee with a large horn of dry, sweet biscuit, another that he fetch her reticule, out of which would soon tumble a little roll of *lire*, which he would always return.

Not a one of them could be below the age of nine-and-forty, and despite individually excellent features—fine dark eyes on one, a perfect small Grecian nose on another, shell-like ears on the third—none were even equivocally beautiful, wide as that word had been stretched for Addison in the past. Nevertheless, they seemed shrewd. They knew well what went on in the town, and who came and went through the town, and their palaver might soon be of value to him, so he was unfailingly polite. But no, the Signora F. decided that he was too conspicuous to be a confederate, *grazie*.

To them all, he had continued to express the pathos-drenched legend that his somewhat ungracious aunt was about to visit, and perhaps all too aware of his economically straightened situation, she might be actively eschewing him. The kind-hearted, gossipy, lightly moustached *signoras* empathized with Addison, having no doubt been out of pocket themselves due to some handsome scoundrel in their own day. To a woman, they vociferously promised to alert him to the arrival of anyone even vaguely English or aunt-like in the town, and, if necessary, to help persuade her to his cause. But so far, no luck had crowned their alleged vigilance.

Then as he was leaving for an afternoon stroll, suddenly next to him outside the front of the pensione, there was the *Avvocato*, who not only greeted him by name, but placed a grey-gloved hand upon his forearm in a surprisingly intimate gesture and asked in quite good English if *Il Inglese* had a few moments to look at something the *Avvocato* had in his home.

Curious if this was a come-on or what, exactly, Addison agreed to accompany him. The lawyer lived above his law chambers, and while it was large, with many bright, airy rooms, he couldn't help notice how under-furnished it was, by comparison with not only the *Pensione Ercoli* but virtually every other home in Ancona he'd peered into. The library was no better furnished, with only a large old desk and a single chair. The walls were bare of pictures, yet their square, rectangular, and in one case, oval, outlines were still visible, all suggestive of a man whose financial star had waned over the past nine decades and who was selling off what he or his ancestors had accumulated.

The first small recto volume Marcellini drew out for Addison's perusal was a printed volume in Latin and Greek, which Addison recognized but neither read nor spoke.

"Lucretius," the lawyer declared. "Very early. Sixteen hundred and ten."

The second volume was larger by far and contained ink drawings with at places blushes of colour, representing several youths and young women partly dressed and then undressed, and then actively engaged in various sensual activities. This looked far more modern. Addison was about to ask if the lawyer was the artist, when he saw the profile of a hawk-nosed youth with an unmistakably protruding lower lip upon which rested a portion of another youth's member. Several other drawings confirmed that the lawyer, albeit much younger, was well represented.

"I am told you are in the employ of a great lord," Marcellini said.

"You are told correctly."

"Art of this sort is not so common, I believe, in England."

"Never common enough, especially when it is so… variegated. You are certain you can part with this?"

"Ah, yes. Everyone who is modelled is dead," he glibly lied.

"Then, yes. I shall write to him about these two volumes. This larger one might interest him greatly."

The lawyer then handed Addison a sheet of pre-printed paper which contained his name, several academic degrees, and an office address.

"I shall write to him first by telegraph, if that suits you," Addison said. "It is faster."

He was about to step out of the room when a ray of sun caught a particular section of the by now thinning books on a shelf behind the desk. Always one for signs, Addison followed it and found a few more Latin texts and a curious notebook of some dark animal hide but almost paper thin from much handling. Within it was handwritten correspondence in very fine, even fading ink-cursive between two friends. One superscription was that of an Umberto Achille Marcellini, doubtless the lawyer himself, in 1823. But the other, while not as readily legible, was somehow familiar.

"And is this for sale?" Addison said. "It seems to be the intimate letters of two young men. That Grecian kind of relationships interests both myself and my lord. Would you sell it to us?"

The lawyer looked startled at first, perhaps by the volume even coming to light, then he seemed ever so briefly enraged, and then resigned.

"Yes, for a very dear price."

"Then I will certainly mention it in my telegram. I'll go do that now."

The lawyer directed him to the centre of Ancona, where the telegraph station was located. On his way, Addison had a thought. Didn't one of the card-playing signoras tell him she had been left a large number of English-language books by guests? It wouldn't be unnatural for him to call upon her and ask to see them.

It turned out she was just returned home from the *Pensione Ercoli* card game herself and was surprised and flattered he'd called on her. She had her girl bring him more coffee—this one foamy and called *macchiato*—and let him peruse her left-behind-by-guests library.

He flung open the little compendium of British poets she had, and there he found the plate of the bust he was looking for as well as his not too unfamiliar signature. Upon another page, he found a full-length portrait which showed the great man in detail, so cleverly achieved that the viewer scarcely made out the club foot. Doubtless the same club foot being licked by several women in those ink drawings the *Avvocato* had shown him. The same club foot being thrust up to the tarsal-knuckles into the anus of one of the other young men. Oh, yes! That *would* be a find! Letters and drawings of the young Lord Byron! He wondered if he should even let His Lordship look at the letters once he had them in hand. Surely the drawings ought to be enough to hold his interest.

>   9 October 188—
>   Casa Ippolito Nuovo,
>   Ancona, Italy

My Lord,
   My landlady knocked on the door and told me a train filled with passengers is coming in from Lake Garda, the first such in four days. Perhaps my great Aunt—for so have I styled Her L-ship to the woman—is on the train? If I hurry, I can meet it at the station. And so My Lord, I go. And drop these lines in a post-box as I do.
   Yrs.
   Addison Grimmins

>   12 October 188—
>   Late of the Pensione Ercoli
> Current: Palazzo Di Moderi, Calle Albinoni
>   Venice, Italy

My Lord,
   As you will note from the above postal address, I've gone ahead into Venice itself. Several days of waiting about the railroad station at Ancona proved fruitless.
   At my arrival at the railroad terminal in Venice several hours later, I located a telegraph office and sent you the note you should have already received.
   Yrs.
   Addison Grimmins

❖

It was a nuisance, he had to admit. And his own fault. Once he'd mentioned the old man's volume of letters to the Signora Faschiletti and somehow made it transparent to her how desirable the object would be for him to obtain, she'd replied, "Come late, after the twelve of the clock to my rooms. Knock twice low on the door, and I will give you the lire. Then you may pay me back."

Well, the money was certainly there, but so was the signora herself, in a rather picturesque *déshabillé*, her hair down, a mere touch of rouge on her lips, and perhaps even on the tips of her breasts. So, the invitation appeared to a fellow of his sophistication to be more like a command performance. As it had been more than a few days since his most recent Teutonic activities, Addison performed commandingly. He was out of the signora's chambers and into his own by two of the clock.

No sooner had he awakened that morning than he saw the note under his door. Not a *billet-doux* as he'd feared, but a visiting card from a Mr. Worthley of the Thos. Cook & Son Travel Office, notifying him that the wire order of funds from His Lordship had arrived and could be obtained at certain hours.

The usual *caffe latte* and almond-filled bun for breakfast with no sign of his recent *innamorata* and he was out the door. Worthley was in the office as promised, and Old Marcellini was up early, too. He was quick to hand over the three volumes, which he then aided Addison in wrapping in parcel paper. For a minute before departing, Addison thought he ought to say something indicating *what* he believed he knew. But then he thought better of it and simply half bowed and withdrew. After this transaction, the old man wouldn't need to sell any more furniture or pictures or books if he lived on another decade of need, which seemed all too likely.

But when Addison reached the Thos. Cook & Son office again, and was looking over the parcels, he was surprised to find a folded note on Marcellini's printed notepaper, and a scrawled message. *It is no sin to be beautiful. It is no sin to give love.*

"Indeed, sir! You have hit the nail on the head!" Addison said.

"Pardon?" Worthley looked up from his wrapping, baffled.

"Never you mind! But *do* mind your packing of these two valuable objects is redundant to a fault."

"Not to worry, sir. We know our business."

Addison returned to the *Pensione Ercoli*, packed his bag, and brought it downstairs to what passed for a business desk in the vestibule. With the infamous third volume in hand opening up so many new possibilities, it seemed high time to leave the boring little town.

She was there, prim and proper this morning as only a satisfied woman could be. All business.

"I fear, Signora, that I can no longer await my aunt, but must move on."

"It is high time for it," she said tersely. Her two hulking nephews were in sight and hearing, lounging in the vestibule.

"Il conto, Signora?" he asked, putting his long wallet on the counter.

"Here it is, Sir Inglese."

He was looking it over and surprised that it was merely a bill for the time he had spent at the place, with several meals discounted, and no sign at all of the "loan" of the night before.

"No added special fares?" he asked, to be certain.

"The charming company of Sir Inglese, for myself and my *cumadres* at our little entertainments, has any special fare taken away."

"*Grazie, Signora. Molto gentile.*"

"*Prego.* But you should know then, Sir Inglese, that the son of my *cumadre* Maria-Grazia believes he has seen just such a lady as you have to us descripted. Your *Gran-Tia*? And also, a little *donna* he believed *Italiana o Francese*."

"No?" He tried not to appear utterly dumbfounded. "When was this?"

"*Sì*, Sir Inglese. Yesterday. With them, younger men. I only this morning have report."

"*Grazie, Signora.* Did your *cumadre*'s son by any chance discover where in Ancona my aunt lodges?"

"No here. To Venezia they go. *Pronto!* Aunt. *Donna. Uomini.* All. By the train. Darkest night."

When he was bedding her. It made a certain madcap sense.

For a second, he wondered how long she had intended to keep this information from him. Perhaps not until after he'd ceased creeping into her bedroom after midnight.

"*Grazie*, once again. I shall not fail to recommend this lodging to all Englishmen."

"Then one more thing for to know," she said. "This *Ercoli*," referring to the fresco of the muscular Greek hero Hercules behind her desk and indeed pictures on many elements of the *pensione*, including his bill, "He was for it pose, *amico lei—il Vecchio!*" Her nose pointed out the door.

"*Il Avvocato* Marcellini posed for this?" he asked.

"Not him. His friend. The poet."

He stared, and sure enough, the club foot was hidden by the pose.

His Lordship would have paid immensely for a photograph of this muscular nude pose had the medium existed when the fresco was made. But it had been a quarter century too early for photography.

But that meant she knew all about the old man.

"The poet?"

"It's true. We are very proud, all this Ancona."

So, they must all know! Perhaps not uneducated Jessica, the maid. But all the *cumadres* knew!

Addison bowed to her. She half curtseyed to him.

As he swung his bag out the door, one of the nephews all but lifted him into a gaily decorated little one-horse gig headed to the train station.

❖

At his arrival at the railroad terminal in Venice, he located a tiny telegraph office and sent another telegram confirming his arrival and that the volumes had been sent off. The trip had been long, a dozen hours, and uneventful unless one counted the assorted domestic animals which had to be removed from the track and at one point where the trestle crossed a small river, many people cackled about the love-suicide by drowning of a local young lady.

By now it was evening, and the train was the last of the day to arrive in the large, still fairly new terminal. The usual noise and smoke and shouts of porters and equally loud replies of passengers, the exclamations of greeters and of those being greeted were all slowly fading away. Addison had no desire to do anything more than sit at a spindly metal table with the greenish glass top, patterned like the waves of the sea, dandling a small glass of French brandy and a larger glass of carbonated water as he got his bearings and tried to see what, or who, would be of use to him in this new location.

For the most part, the terminal workers and railroad men

were concerned with finishing their jobs and closing up their various businesses and going home. Even the bartender of this little *enoteca*, or wine shop, was washing down his shelves and counting his cash. They didn't count in Addison's book, and neither did any of the straggling passengers, since those that he sought had surely come and gŏne earlier in the morning. But he had learned—and not only from the example of his lord— that a simple "look 'round" could reveal miracles, or at least potentialities, if one remained both observant and sufficiently collected in his wits.

It was then that he spotted one of those layabout lads who sometimes earn small change helping people with their bags, and sometimes earn slightly larger amounts pocketing unattached objects that came into their vicinity. This lad reminded Addison of himself not too long ago, albeit less angelic in appearance than charmingly fox-like, with his narrow, light green eyes and dark blond hair, as well as his slender form. His bleached-out coloured jacket, blouse, and trousers, not to mention his cheap rope and leather footwear or the oh-so-studied casual indifference he affected, marked him as that type. It came in all nationalities.

This layabout spotted Addison spotting him. He rose leisurely and ambled past the spindly little table twice, the second time asking indifferently, *"Cicerone? Signor?"* Meaning did he need a guide.

"Cuanto lingue parla?" It turned out he spoke two languages, French and Italian. But also a spattering of Austrian and English—i.e., more than enough for Addison, whose Italian had grown by leaps and bounds in the past week, thanks to the card-playing landladies. So Addison pointed to his *portmanteau*, locked tight, the key around his neck.

The layabout lad lifted it easily, and as Addison finished his apertif with a final toss, he was led outside the terminus to a dark and somewhat wet street chemically redolent of that atmospheric pause between rain showers and to a waiting taxi: one of those one passenger single-horse types so popular in the narrow streets of the canal-crossed city. He of course had led Addison directly to some relative or confederate of his, attached to an ancient jade of a nag and a worn suede cabriolet, but Addison demurred, stopping suddenly at a café table, sitting and calling for one of those poisonous little two-sip *demitasses* which became heavenly with the addition of a spoonful of anise-flavoured sugar and a twist of lemon.

His layabout lad was cool enough to wait, but when he began to hunker down on his heels by the table, Addison insisted he rise and sit like a man. He purchased for him a *gelato amandine*. There, at the tiny table, while Luca bathed his delightful face in the iced dessert, Addison probed him as gently as he knew how.

What had Luca's friends told him? Addison was certain all those unofficially employed about the station exchanged information, so that they might more easily identify their robbery victims.

"An early train from Switzerland brought a half dozen foreigners. Some noble, some not."

"Was a great lady among them? Traveling with a chaperone and chamber maid?"

"I believe so. My friend said—"

"Did your friend overhear which *albergo* they were going to?"

No hotel, it turned out. They were met by a private carriage, which had certain scrolls indicative of the local nobility on its sides, and which moved so quickly his friends were not able to know where.

"I could find out tomorrow," he insisted. And here the lad realized he had foolishly released the crucial information

Addison sought without first asking a fee. He became so transparently disappointed by his error that Addison forestalled his departure by saying he would, after all, require Luca's services as *cicerone* for the following few days. But first he was to bring Addison to excellent lodgings, but *not* owned or operated by a relative. And he was to return there in the morning.

Luca was all smiles again, and it was as though the sun had just come out from behind a cloud. As for the information he furnished, only one lady had recognizably spoken English *in his presence* among the past few day's arrivals. She had travelled not in a large suite but with a single, tall, stout man around thirty-five or forty years of age, who had looked about himself very cautiously. Amidst the departing passengers all around them, the stout fellow had conveyed them into a gondola to take them to a palazzo beyond the Rialto. This had occurred the previous evening, far too early for the woman Addison was seeking.

Meanwhile, Luca thought he knew of the woman he'd been told to look out for, the same party that his Ancona landlady's *cumadre*'s son had described. At least he knew her to be different. She had distinctly spoken English but also French, he'd been told, and her party was another woman with, perhaps, a younger man.

However, Luca temporized even that by saying she was a great lady, already known to him by repute. The Comtesse de St. Roche-Debreville.

Addison immediately distinguished her as a great London friend of his lord, one whom he'd been honoured to be introduced to in his company some two years past.

To test this theory and Luca's veracity and usefulness, he waited until they had arrived by a more official-looking gondola at a hotel whose name he recognized had been on a "recommended" list in the *Baedeker Guide* he'd possessed himself of as well upon a list at the Thos. Cook & Son office. Once settled in his chamber, he sat down and enclosed his lord's calling card, along with his own hasty note on the establishment's stationery, in a single envelope and gave it to Luca to present at the Comtesse's address.

Luca was as though magically transformed into Addison's boon confederate by the possibility of his knowing such a highborn and affluent Lady. Luca returned within the half hour, as Addison was unpacking his belongings.

I'll be most put out, Comtesse Diane wrote, *if you* don't *come tomorrow and keep me company in this draughty, old, waterlogged palace while you are in Venice.*

After his scanty breakfast the following morning, Addison paid her a visit accompanied by Luca. The Comtesse greeted him on the second level, the floor they called *piano* here. The rooms were too wide and too long, the furniture too large and very old, and, to his taste, quite ugly. But the weather had cleared to a sparkling blue sky, and the remains of the previous day's rain lay in puddles on roofs and added to the general glitter of the foliage as they sat outside on a tiny balcony.

"They call virtually everything with four walls and a roof a *palazzo* here," the Comtesse assured him over a pot of Assam tea with an assortment of little sandwiches. "Including this monstrosity. But I suppose it was such a creature at one time or another."

"Why not ask its owner?"

"I *am* its owner. Which I am reminded of whenever repairs are required, which is often enough." She laughed.

She was charming, he decided. Dressed in what was an up-to-the-throat frock of simple but surely expensive materials tailored for her. Perfectly appropriate for a lady to entertain a single gentleman, her chestnut hair tumbling out of its fixture in back, down and onto one shoulder. In London, she had seemed as artificial as any other socialite, with the usual excessive amount of ribbons, laces, furbelows, and cosmetics. But here, she scarcely wore a blush of colour around her sky-matching eyes or rouge on her perfectly delineated lips.

"That being the case, Madame, should I accept your invitation to take up residence here, I'm afraid the neighbours would have much to say."

"They certainly would. I'm counting on them doing so. In hasty, ungrammatical telegrams flying back across the Alps." And when he looked surprised, she added, "That is where my lover and my husband both are, and it would do them a world of good to remind them that I am here with another, younger, dashing young man like yourself."

"Should they arrive, Comtesse, I foresee scenes. Duels on abandoned islands."

"You see far more than I," she said. "Knowing them as I do, it might take an assassin's explosive to get them off their well-bred rears." They sipped, they nibbled. "Now who is that mite you have deposited downstairs to bewitch my servant girls?"

"My man, Luca."

"Your man! Aren't you both adorable!" Before he could protest, she said in deeper tones. "So, who is this person you have crossed Europe to overtake?"

"I'm not entirely certain I can reveal her name."

"Posh! It must be Lillian, Marchioness of R——, who has absconded and about time too, I say. Close your mouth, Mr. Grimmins. While your teeth are gratifyingly clean, it is still an unseemly posture in mixed company with no dental professional in view."

"How many know?"

"More than Lord R. would like. Not that many, but it is

better that some *do know*. How else will you find her? Certainly not by either of our mites' gathered intelligence reports. She's certain to show herself in society here, where she may believe she is safe."

"So you believe."

"I do. The lad downstairs doesn't look very strong or very bad. Neither do you, Mr. Grimmins. Please forgive me. At least I hope not. Whereas Venice is filled with unsavoury and trustworthy bravos for hire."

"Well, then, actually locating the Marchioness will suffice. You will aid me in that?"

"Why not? It's a few larks more than I expected, coming here. But you must be my male companion while we are out of doors together."

"I'm not a gentleman."

"You'll do, as I have no chaperone. For form's sake. Your mite can linger after us."

"For form's sake, then?"

"Yes. I'm ever in need of discreet British company."

Agreed. With pleasure.

16 October 188—
Palazzo Di Moderi, Calle Guardi
Venice, Italy

My Lord,

    The Comtesse with whom I now reside in Venice bids me write to you of her plans to travel to England in a few months and wishes to be certain you will visit her at G—— House in Surrey when she does so. She kindly asked that I might attend you there, as she has come to "value your company, you rapscallion, you!"

    As you will doubtless assume, ever eager in your service, sir, I have divided my amatory efforts into the staff—the young Venetian lay-about and spy—and the distaff, Her Grace herself, "ever in need of discreet British company," as she so delicately puts it. My only fear in this, although I am rigorous in my inspection of his parts, is that he poxes me, and I then all unaware shall pox her.

    Our quarry is definitely here. Quite of a sudden, I came upon her big blackguard outside a wine shop. I recognized him as the very fellow who bid me good day in Innsbruck in the snow. So, we have been moving parallel, it seems. I did write that I felt close to Her Ladyship, you may recall. If I only knew how near!

    This time, I slipped away unnoticed, but my "man" saw him and will thus know him for any future forays. My man once more saw the fellow and watched him carefully enough to see him standing guard one afternoon over an old, well-known, and extremely respectable palazzo, out of which our *quarry herself, or so we believe the woman to be, exited, joining her fellow as he escorted her warily to another, far less exquisite, hotel.*

So I now have two possible addresses for her.

I believe the blackguard to be dangerous and would much prefer managing him out of my direct way to her, whether temporarily or permanently, I am not yet decided. Have you any counsel for me in this matter, I shall of course undertake it.

Yrs.
Addison Grimmins

❖

Luca had only just obtained the second address entered by the lady and her guard when he was accosted by a foreigner, whether British or American he was not sure, but one or the other, he was certain.

He reported the fellow was of middle age, dressed expensively but not gaudily so, high-browed, with a thick, full, brown beard and warm brown eyes, albeit not at all Mediterranean in feature. More importantly, Luca had seen him exit the *palazzo* and signal with a wave to the departing lady, who preceded him by half a minute. This foreigner had then immediately noted Luca's presence not far away observing the scene. He followed Luca for some time, until Luca decided to test the extent of that interest.

He slipped into a narrow alley which held but a bit of land and grass between two *palazzi*, and stood still. At which point the man had looked closely at Luca, looked about himself as though checking whether he himself were being observed, and deciding that was not so, he quickly entered the alley.

Luca had pretended he was about to relieve himself, and

the older man quickly took hold of Luca's manhood and named a price for purchasing his personal services for not very many minutes. Luca said they haggled briefly over precisely which services. This, Luca said, he did in hopes of explaining in mime what he was doing there to begin with, should any curious neighbour actually be watching and require an explanation for Luca's continued presence observing the lady's residence. Also, Luca admitted, he did it to accommodate the fellow, who seemed especially eager. Unspoken was that Luca was already inured to doing that sort of thing for money.

This act proposed and completed, *lire* changed hands, and Luca off-handedly asked the fellow if the woman he'd seen emerge just before the man was the Comtesse LaRoche-Debreville, whom he pretended a friend had told him was in Venice.

"No, the Comtesse is much younger. This lady is older," the man said. Luca thought he seemed amused. "She would be almost a Nonna to you. Does that sort intrigue you?"

"No, no," Luca had responded. His mistake. A misunderstanding. He'd only seen her briefly and from a distance.

But then Luca did ask, "Who was that stalwart *uomo* who walked with her? Her son? Her grandson?"

"Ah! So *he* is who interests you?" the man said, satisfied at last. "But I doubt you would interest *him*. That fellow is merely a countryman of hers. Among her countrymen, ladies of her age and her rank never go about abroad without someone constantly on duty."

Having obtained that information, Luca then feigned indifference. He did however admit to being available on this and a few other *calles* and *vias* in the neighbourhood, in the case of the gentlemen wishing to see him again. And so they parted ways.

Addison then probed Luca about her companion. From watching them together, Luca said he believed the blackguard to be strong and commanding toward her and her maid, and he was dictatorial and dangerously bad-tempered toward servants. Luca believed Addison should much prefer dealing with him away from the lady altogether, whether temporarily or permanently.

❖

"Don't be shy," the Comtesse said. "Come into the room. It's only wardrobes and a few chests. We can't go out to this afternoon's luncheon with you dressed as you usually are. While it isn't a formal affair, it is more or less what passes for daytime society in this dreary city. You'll have to put on something more brilliant than what you have. Come and try on a few of these afternoon coats. The Comte is about your size, and they will only be a little bit loose on you.

"There! Either of those will do. We must work from the boots up, because there you *are* different sizes. Please stand still. Let me loosen and unbutton your shirt and put this lovely handkerchief around your neck. It was a gift. Italian silk. You need not wear a cravat. Move away. Now turn about a bit. Yes, I like how the starry midnight blue of the handkerchief plays with your own blue eyes."

"I am your doll, then. To be clad as you wish," Addison said.

"If only you were, I could do wonders with you! But no, Mr. Grimmins, you are too much your own man. You are merely my daytime chaperone today. If I am to look my best, you must look…well, you must look at least as good as you do now. Go on. Look in the mirror. It won't bite you."

He had looked into enough mirrors and seen enough of

himself in mirrors for various reasons and at various times in his life that he was able to affect being utterly casual about it. But he had to admit he'd never seen *this* Addison Grimmins before. Gone his former incarnation as the deft London city gentleman, although in reality he'd been far more city than he'd been a gentleman. Still, he'd worn that figure adroitly. But this tanned young man, his inky hair unshorn longer than usual and therefore wavy and curling up at its tips in the humid atmosphere, his posture upright and lean yet *soigne*, his clothing careful yet playful—who *was* this fellow?

He had Luca call for a larger than usual gondola, one with a little shade over its poler's end. The three of them rode in it together, Addison and the Comtesse under the awning, Luca in the open. As they approached the house they were to be at, Luca looked all around and suddenly said in Italian, "Right here, the man in brown and I!" pointing to another building with a narrow alleyway between it and its neighbour.

"And there," he added, pointing to a yellow façade ahead, punctuated by third-level balconies with flowers trailing from windowsills and gratings. "Where they visited."

"Unsurprisingly," the Comtesse allowed. "Since that is the Palazzo Inginieri, where the unofficial British hostess of Venice resides. And where our luncheon party lies. Lucky you."

Luca was supposed to remain on the first floor with the other servants but, always original, he waited outside the building, lounging here and sunning himself there, visible to Addison whenever he happened to chance to glance out. This he did seldom enough at first. From the minute he and the Comtesse arrived at the *piano* level and were greeted by their hostess and host, he felt himself on the alert in a way he seldom felt unless he was reporting to Lord R. in person. After all, he was playing a new role today.

Today he was Diane's *cousine*, Addison.

"Isn't he pretty, Christina?" she said. "And he's entirely housebroken. Well, *almost* entirely."

For her part, Christina, the Principessa Pardolini, was thrilled. "This is *not* the Prince," she said to Addison with a clear Somerset accent, indicating the slightly younger man next to her. "That creature is off somewhere hunting other creatures only a little less mythological than himself. Instead, this is my cousin, Brian Rudolf Hetch."

"Of the Highland Hetches," Hetch said, as though Addison would have a clue what that entailed.

Tall, blond, and expressionless, Hetch kept a grip on Addison's hand and turned him aside deftly, speaking in what Addison interpreted as an authentic Scots accent. "We all adore the Comtesse."

"I can understand why you do," Addison said, wondering if that was a warning.

"And a few more new faces. Just up the stairs. Thank you, Mr. Addison, for coming!" the Principessa said. He took the cue and Diane's hand, and they swept up the wide, green and grey swirled marble staircase to the next higher level where the luncheon party was slowly coming together.

More introductions flew fast and furious as he joined the Comtesse in meeting one after another wealthy-looking, titled woman, along with her cousin or nephew or childhood friend. Most if not all the latter were physically attractive and dressed informally yet richly in tartans, tweeds, and soft Italian woollens. He'd barely met half of them when the Principessa and her co-host ascended and all followed them into another large chamber, which was set up for lunch.

Once they were all seated at the glittering table with its setting of four plates, four glasses, and a small armoury of silverware, Diane turned to him and said, "If you are unsure, follow my lead." But he wasn't at all unsure, having been taught table manners and more by others even before he'd been in Lord R.'s service. A bell was tinkled and four servants with large tureens of soup appeared as though by magic.

"We all of us wondered," the elderly bejewelled diner to Addison's right said, "when Diane would settle down." As though having a husband and lover was not enough to be settled, Addison thought.

He allowed himself a smile. "Alas, I am merely a cousin, and unfortunately for us both, I will be moving on soon."

He thought she looked surprised at that. "Should you ever find yourself returned to Venice and without a cousin, I insist you come to Ca' Zufanelli. I'm always at home."

He was still wondering how much he had revealed to her for that offer to be made, when she added, "What do you think of this soup? Heavenly, isn't it? They use those honeyed Tuscan cantaloupes."

Ah, that's what it was! A cold broth of melon. Who would have thought it?

For the second course, there was a seafood salad. For the third, medallions of veal. Little dishes to wash one's hands. Then a dessert of black, blue, and raspberries soaked in brandy atop little planks of yellow stuff Diane said was a kind of meal made of maize called polenta.

He'd been careful to take only a few sips of each wine served, and so when the Principessa stood up and announced that the ladies were stepping into the adjoining parlour, he also stood, and asked, "Do I join you?" To which Diane shook her head.

He allowed himself to chat with several of the men, then went over to the window, although he wasn't, like some of them, smoking.

At first, he didn't see Luca. Then he did, almost directly

below and munching on what looked like a dishful of *maccheroni*. However, he was alert. Luca looked up, saw him, put down the food, and pointed to the building with both index fingers, signifying inside. Someone had arrived. Luca then made a curved figure with his hands, covering his face—a veiled woman. Then he put his hands out facing each other and moving them up and down, signifying a man. In turn, Addison gestured as to where, and Luca counted to two. On the second, or *piano* floor.

Suddenly, a fellow from the luncheon party was at Addison's side. "Tell me, young sir, from where do we know each other? You seem so familiar, and yet I can't for the life of me place you."

"I'm sorry but I don't recall your name. Were we introduced?"

"No, but you were introduced to my wife, Lady Etheridge, as you and the Comtesse came in." Addison *did* recall the man, one whose bedroom he'd frequented at a house party in Sussex.

"Not Tony Ducliffe, Lord Etheridge?" Addison asked, already knowing the answer. "Addison Grimmins. Lately employed in the office of Milord the Marquis of R——."

Tony began to blush, and Addison knew he'd remembered exactly *where* they'd met. "I see we have both prospered since that time."

"Haven't *we* ever?" Addison said, remembering how, after their pairing, Tony told him how badly his finances were and how he needed to be "caught" by one of the heiresses that weekend. Clever Tony. He *had* been caught.

He suspected Tony was about to ask for an encore of that night, so he quickly excused himself, went to the parlour door, found Diane, and managed to get her attention and point downstairs.

"Her?" the clever woman asked in mime.

"Maybe?" he gestured back.

She finished her conversation *à trois*, excused herself, and, finding him, said, "Where?"

"The next level down."

"You're certain?"

"Of course not. But I must go look."

"Of course you must. Here's what we'll do." She outlined a simple plan in which she would wander around, allegedly looking for a water closet. If she didn't return in a certain time, he would come after her. She'd been in this *palazzo* before, and with a Prosecco-dipped finger upon a banquette, she outlined the floor plan for him and which rooms to follow in what order. "There is a water closet down there," she assured him. "But, if I linger more than a few minutes, you come after me."

Not ten minutes later, Addison excused himself from further conversation with the bejewelled older woman who'd been at his right at dinner, saying, "I believe the washroom is down here?" But before going back down, he asked if he might take a look through the *pince-nez* she had hanging by a thin gold chain.

"It looks perfect on you," she declared. "Can you see anything at all through the glass?"

"Surprisingly, I can see very well."

"My eyes are not so bad. And only the left one is off."

"Might I borrow it a few minutes while I'm downstairs?"

"I've got another pair," she said with a shrug. "You can keep it."

A glance in the mirror with the *pince-nez* on told Addison he'd now added another level of disguise.

Diane's floor plan had been accurate, and he moved from drawing room to drawing room before he finally espied the stalwart back of the blackguard. He stopped dead, wondering what next when he heard the Comtesse to his left say, "Here's my cousin now."

She half stood from out of a *fauteuil* next to a double window. In front of the windows was a loveseat, and in it was—well, it was *her*, wasn't it? Alone on the sofa, dressed in cobalt blue with a light veil lifted aside from her face onto a small grey cap.

"Come meet a countrywoman of ours also visiting Venice," Diane said, making a funny face at him because, he was certain, of the glasses he wore. "My cousin is rather bookish and hopelessly shy, which really won't do in Venice," she said to the Marchioness. "But then he is young and completely unaccustomed to our manners on the Continent."

"My pleasure." Addison was certain the Marchioness would recognize him as he half bowed to take her hand in its pale blue lacework glove. From this close she looked different, more free somehow, more relaxed certainly, and yet it *was* her. They'd meet and then what? "Lady…?" He turned to the Comtesse for a hint.

"Mrs. Smith," the Marchioness said.

"Mrs. Smith."

"Mrs. Smith is staying here at Ca' Ingineri, but was just retiring for the afternoon," Diane said. "Please don't let us hinder you."

The Marchioness stood up, and her blackguard suddenly moved in to accompany her, throwing a half-questioning, half-disdainful glance at Addison, who turned toward the Comtesse and affected not to know him or to notice he'd been the focus of his observation.

They waited until the two were out of sight, then Diane said. "It was *her*. I only met her once, but I'm certain."

"It was *definitely* her. But do you think she knew it was me?"

"You're joking. *I* barely knew it was *you!*" she said with a laugh. She led them to a floor-length pier glass built into one wall.

"Look for yourself. With those—don't they call them peepers in America—you are completely changed somehow."

He bussed her soft cheek, watching himself in the glass as he did so. He looked like no Addison he'd ever seen before, or had ever expected to see. "Mrs Smith" would have had to be a brilliant detective to recognize Lord R.'s security man from England.

"So now," Diane asked as they went over to the grand staircase where the luncheon party was finishing itself in departures, "now, are you content? Can you now report back to your lord that you have tracked down his traveling distaff?"

"Completely." Addison didn't totally lie. "But now I'm wondering how in the world I could possibly begin to thank you. Do any ideas come to mind?"

19 October 188—
Palazzo Di Moderi, Calle Guardi
Venice, Italy

My Lord,

You will, I hope, be gratified to learn at long last that conversance has been achieved between myself as your agent and Her Ladyship! She did not appear at all to have made the connexion between the surly fellow in black garb who was on guard at the wedding festivities in Cumbria and this more colourful figure that I cut in demi-disguise. Nor did I in any manner allow her to do so, thinking it still imprudent.

The scene was an afternoon luncheon at a local Palazzo attended by various British of high birth and their assorted companions. Not that Her L-ship was in any way on display. To the contrary, she was virtually hidden and had to be sought out. Your—and now my own—resourceful friend, the Comtesse, provided the means for that. It was but the briefest of connexions. How to get closer for a longer amount of time remains the problem. Her Cerberus was only a yard distant, as usual. Getting him separated further or for good is the next logical step. I am not yet decided of which means to invoke in doing so.

As you can infer, My Lord, our nets slowly enclose them.

Yr. Servant
Addison Grimmins

❖

It was almost bedtime when Luca tapped on his chamber door. "He goes out soon, as I told you. Again. We follow now? You and I?"

"Since you insist," Addison said, quickly dressing for the outdoors in darker and heavier clothing. It had been another sparkling beautiful day in the city, but just before sunset, a large storm cloud had moved in, hovering over the nearby streets. Suddenly, it began precipitating. He hugged himself more closely within his heavy mariner's coat, and Luca, ever the native, rewrapped the woollen scarf Addison had thrown to him more closely around his neck and shoulders.

One of Luca's relations was their awaiting gondolier, and his craft was a slender bullet of a boat, moving so rapidly Luca barely had time to ring a bell in warning whenever they approached or crossed another canal as they must do at night to avoid collisions.

In mere minutes, they were at the Ca' Inginieri, and another relation, seeing them slip into place at a wall-pier across from the *palazzo*, held up five fingers to Luca and then added two more.

"He comes out in seven minutes," Luca whispered.

"He is that regular?"

"He does it every night."

Addison lifted out his pointer; the little fob watch read ten minutes past midnight. He watched the minutes pass, and in time heard the tinkle of the bell on Luca's relation's gondola. Out of the shadowy *palazzo* doorway stepped the blackguard, tall, dressed in black, and moving rapidly.

He spoke Italian in too low a voice for them to hear, but he quickly got in the other gondola, and Luca's relation was already poling them into the centre of the canal.

His own gondolier waited until they were just in sight, and then he poled them out in deeper water where he would make less noise and be less conspicuous. As they followed, Luca hung over the front, a partly shaded lantern in hand.

Although he carefully noted every turn, Addison was soon lost. The other craft's own orange-gold half-light ahead was often obscured by sudden mists, and once by two other larger craft crossing in between. At times, his gondolier suddenly stopped and listened, after which he would furiously pole them ahead. From one side or the other, they would hear two or three people laughing in darkness, or someone moaning from some dim alleyway, whether with pain or pleasure was never clear.

Whenever they would stop, he heard water splashing against one unknown object or another from one indistinguishable source or another. As they sped along, the walls danced in reflections, rising and declining in little wavelets. Eventually the canals they entered became narrower and longer, and the light in the gondola ahead drew steadier, even as sudden sheets of fog dropped to enclose them so as to not allow them to see a foot around.

His boatman stopped suddenly, and they heard a scraping of the side of the other boat's bowhead against a wall.

"Now!" Luca said, and their boatman guided them into a wall with a half stairway up.

"On foot now!" Luca said, leaping out and up. He turned and threw a hand down to Addison.

Ahead of them, the figure got out of the gondola and said something.

"He wants my friend to wait for him," Luca said. They heard coins clanging onto the gondola's flat wooden bottom.

Luca kept himself close to the walls, mostly because there was sporadic light from building entryways and even at one corner a duo of what looked like carriage lanterns from an earlier, more ornate century fixed atop twelve-foot poles driven into the ground. Two cats squalled ahead and then screeched as the shadow Addison and Luca followed either trod upon or kicked them. They heard him mutter dark imprecations. Ahead they could make out the calls and responding replies of small groups of revellers, but before they could reach this canal, they split off at a tangent and he heard them celebrating deep into another *via*.

The blackguard stopped ahead. Addison could see his figure clearly now. Stopped, looking ahead.

"Where are we?" he asked Luca in a whisper.

"You see that arch and gate? This leads into *Il Ghetto*."

"Which is what?"

"Where the Papa meant for the Jews-people to live."

"The Papa? Oh! You mean the Pope! As exiles? For their safety? Or what?"

Luca shrugged. "All, perhaps."

"He comes here every night?"

"Every night."

"He meets a woman here? A Jewess?"

Luca shrugged. "No. He stands. Then he goes back."

So he did again. He stood for maybe ten minutes, then rushed back to his gondola, taking the boatman by surprise. He shouted at him to wake up and return him to the *palazzo*.

The boat swept past and Addison caught a glimpse of the big man's face, half covered by his own large hand, facing down into the gondola's bottom, in anguish or... Addison didn't know what, but clearly disturbed within the light of the gondola's lantern. Then it was gone.

"He returns now?" Addison asked.

"Every night," Luca said once more.

Well. It was a mystery. But mysteries required solutions.

"Remain here!" Addison walked slowly ahead until he'd reached the very spot where the blackguard had stood.

Ahead was the arch with some lettered inscription in Latin, which he could not read, and also in what he recognized as Hebrew. It looked like an ordinary street within the gate, with four- and five-storey buildings on either side and occasional street lamps, all of it vacant of life and gleaming wet. A few windows with grilles looked out directly to the canal, all of them unlighted. What could possibly be here, to draw the man night after night?

Whatever it was, this forlorn site did provide a potential spot for mayhem, whether mere assault or more. He wasn't certain whether he could depend upon Luca for anything like that. He rather suspected not. But surely the man would know of some—bravos, Diane called them—to put the fellow out of commission, in hospital at the least. Would the Marchioness then remain huddled in the *palazzo*? No, she had to come out sometime, and that's when she could be snatched.

He had turned around slowly during these ruminations and was walking away from the ghetto arch when his olfactory sense was suddenly alerted to a new aroma. Well, not so new, as not unfamiliar. Once it had been familiar by association, and not to him directly but to someone he'd once encountered. Who?

He followed it through the mist into a short *via* that dead-ended away from the ghetto arch. He found himself in front of a shoddy tenement, but the smell was gone. Then the doorway opened and two thin women came out, wretchedly clothed and poorly shod, all but clasping each other to stay erect. Not women of the night, but as they passed him, the aroma from before did too, wafting off their clothing, as though soaked into it. And now it was the unmistakeable dragon curling incense of Chinese opium! The Cerberus must know someone who—or wait! No, he must himself *be* an opium addict!

23 October 188—
Answer: Post Restante
Venice, Italy

My Lord,
They are gone, all three of them, and I must guess where to!

Surely they debarked in darkness and by very late or very early hours, because not myself nor my confederates witnessed them leave. My layabout lad for hire came much in use here and earned his pay well. We went about the railroad yards, such as they are, and there, by simple bribery, obtained a direction and time of departure. We go now after them, awaiting a train upon the other shore of Venice and then across the great valley of the River Po. These trains and stations are so small, it will be easy to follow them. Few but local people travel on such small trains, and the three must be conspicuous.

But the fewer travellers here means I should be better able to take advantage of the blackguard's first moment off guard to remove him from the equation altogether.

This I promise to do as soon as can be done. I still await the fate of the Lady herself. Does your continued silence on this important matter mean that you are yourself not yet decided, My Lord? Or is it rather that you await the tenor of politics within London to decide you?

Yr Servant
Addison Grimmins.

❖

He wondered, of course, if he had gone too far in that most recent missive back to Whitehall. But for his peace of mind, never mind his further activity in the matter, he needed to know exactly where he stood and what Lord R.'s intentions actually were. More than once, he'd been complimented to others of Lord R.'s employ as being one who "follows my intentions to the letter." Well, wasn't this now exactly what he did *not* possess, Lord R.'s intention to the letter? He'd been told to follow after Her Ladyship and find her. He had done so, and although she had moved on to this other town, he was certain he'd have her again within an arm's reach. But where *was* the letter with Lord R.'s intentions?

The small train, which would be called a "milk train," brought him and Luca to a terminus at Florence. Addison's farewell to Diane, Le Comtesse, took place late at night in her boudoir, after which he'd slipped out and into his own chamber. There he had packed, including those few pieces of the count's clothing he worn that she'd insisted he take as mementoes, and there he'd set his pointer to repeat quite early, letting the Italian sleep on the carpet in front of his bed. As Addison supposed most younger men did here, Luca awakened rather early and had them and their bags out of the *palazzo* and into a relation's *gondola* in minutes. The *gondola* to the railroad yard, and then on to the train.

Nor was he surprised when Luca said, "I come also."

"You're certain?"

"There, too, Luca has *famiglia.* And large aid to Sir Grimmins."

"I'm no sir, Luca. But of course, you are useful and welcome." So he secured another rail ticket for what passed for first class on the dinky little four-car train. Luca once more proved his use by slipping away while the compartment was being filled, and returning with another relation who had a wicker basket containing little cups he filled with *macchiato*, and napkins he wrapped around some sort of warm bread containing ham and cheese.

    The pottery was handed back out as the little steam locomotive started up with a jerk and slowly pulled away. It would do that a score of times in what didn't even pass for a town before Addison lost count. Luca meanwhile slept the sleep he'd missed and then some.

    Addison tried to do the same, but he had a two-day-old, single-sheet newspaper that served the British and American community that he'd snatched out from under a diner at a restaurant last night. He'd read a headline, "Government Trembles." He waited until he had all of his faculties, and then today on the train, he read with some but without full understanding, he had to admit, but with some foreboding. It was all about the "current occupants of Ten Downing Street, Whitehall," and some other office he was unfamiliar with being "on the alert for a vote of no-confidence being bruited about in the House of Commons. With the Peers remaining aloof when not actually indifferent." The reason for all this was assumed to the reader, but never specifically given, so he wasn't able to follow very well, knowing so few of the names involved.

    What he could do was go to the Thos. Cook & Son office in Florence immediately upon arrival and get updated news, a better understanding—if possible—and as much in the way of Lord R.'s available or already wired in-funds as he could in the event the governmental "trembling" turned into shakes, and worse, into an actual earthquake that tumbled them all. Although being with Diane he'd been able to hold on to his usual weekly cash allotment, he had no intention of having to do without it while several thousand miles from the paymaster in the City of Westminster.

Those thoughts, however, were soon surpassed by the countryside outside the train's windows, which was remarkably varied and quite beautiful. Every little farm house or stable yard or grain barn was picturesque to some extent. The landscape itself changed from coastal villages to little cisalpine towns and then into a broad alluvial plain where numberless dark specks on a fuzzed greyish cloth were actually women up to their knees in water picking what Luca assured him was rice shoots, that Oriental grain quickly adapted to the Mediterranean land.

Over the next stretch of ribbed low mountains and hills, rain showers became animated deluges aimed at their little car. When he delved into his bag for his Marine coat, he found a note from the Comtesse, with her card and what he had to assume was the address of one of her homes in England. With it was a simple gold linked bracelet she'd made him wear their most recent night out.

"You look so severe without it," she'd said. "Look around, every man here has some golden gee-gaw. You might as well be a cleric. And we both know very well that you aren't!"

Also in the bag was a small, beautifully bound and gold-tipped-leaved book, *Two Stories by Mrs. Gaskell*. He opened it to the frontispiece where those two were delineated as "Cousin Phyllis" and "Half A Life Time Ago." A fine ink inscription read, *You are clever enough to enjoy these and lover enough to be moved by them.*

He began reading the first little novel after one stop in which *contadinas* came to the stopped cars with warm milk, wine, and a type of vegetable sandwich they called *panini* and *crostini* which Luca showed him how to eat. And he was indeed touched by the sad tale. He said aloud, "She knows me well." Luca looked up in question. Addison showed him the book and explained what she'd written.

"This great lady you may return to when here you are complete your mission," the younger man said.

"Who told you that?"

"La donna. Tutte lei donne."

But no matter what her servants said, he knew he couldn't possibly feel that way. The Comtesse was married, and her lover was on his way.

Having eaten and drunk wine, Luca began to snooze again. Addison took out his little lap desk, a gift from much earlier in his travels, and looked over those pages he'd scribbled he knew not for whom, some future person of importance. Having read that, he scribbled on, surprised when he looked outside to see that so much time had passed, all he saw was the bare sketch of a sunset, a vague roseate object glowering behind thick strata of clouds.

Luca woke too. "Red sun go down. Tomorrow is no rain." He then lifted himself up to see what was being written.

"It's not about you," Addison said.

"Is to *grand'oumo* in Lon-do-town."

"Perhaps," Addison allowed. Although it was a half ream already, he didn't really know who it was for.

He had finished his writing for the moment when the tracks levelled off and they approached a large town. Sure enough, he heard the sound of double whistles and a conductor's shout, "Fee-ren—zee, Fee-ren—zee."

Once more, Addison waited with his bags at a little café barely inside the terminus while Luca went around gathering information from other young idlers in the place and stopping by periodically for a coffee and update on his progress. He'd taken nearly an hour to properly traduce the local youth of his ilk to provide them with the arrival time and departure for an *osteria* for Her Ladyship and her party. A slightly older female relation had come to meet Luca, and she was able to tell them where their own hotel was and how lucky—*fortunato lei*—Addison was to be able to stay in an *albergo* near it. She would do her best to secure them chambers with front facing windows. Would a three-room suite do?

The lodging of their quarry was a private residence, not a hotel or *pensione*. Luca's cousin thought it belonged to an Englishman's wife, going by the name of Partridge or something similar. Well enough situated, however, not far from the Arno River in a neighbourhood known for large and less old *palazzi*.

Their own residence was across an alley grandly called a *via*. Their parlour room windows looked upon the third storey of that edifice, and insofar as anything *could* be seen, Addison was able to see it.

In this way, within an hour they witnessed Her Ladyship exit with her guard, and Addison quickly got Luca's attention. He was chatting with another clerk there, possibly trying to find out if any jobs were available. The two younger men prudently followed Her Ladyship's party to a private edifice three streets distant where they were received, remained thirty minutes of the hour, and returned again to their lodging.

That evening, Addison and Luca followed the guard as he took off on a postprandial wandering. He crossed over the great old bridge upon which were erected leathercraft and silverworkers' shops with residences all one atop the other, as Addison's familiar London Bridge had used to be ornamented. Once across the river, the fellow passed three times before a house-front which Luca set off to inquire about, while Addison followed the fellow back to his *palazzo*.

It was, as Addison had surmised, an opium den. Evidently, the guard had received the address for this hellhole whilst still in Venice.

Imagine Addison's surprise, when he was walking back

to his lodging house, in coming across his very old friend, Allister MacIlhenny, whom he'd first known as Lobster Tail among the Grimmins Lads, and then as Taurus in the employ of Tiger Jukes in South London. He was standing upon a street corner so casually, he might be back at the southside docks on the Thames and just stopped a minute for a look-around.

"Hello there, lad," Addison said. "Art thou selling thyself?" He had not aged as well as Addison had and looked considerably Addison's senior, although Lobs was dressed better than he could recall, even when he was promoted to Lord R.'s Factor at St. Mary Overy's dock works. By now, his fiery orange hair turned a dull red, along with a little brown goat of a beard. "Or mayhap you're buying tonight?"

Lobster Tail laughed, then wrapped his long arm about Addison's shoulder and led him off to an *enoteca*.

There the two caught up for old time's sake, and Lobster asked what Addison was engaged in. Addison told him he was on a mission for Lord. R., not overstressing any more detailed business.

Lobster then said, "'Ave you seen the little maid?"

"What little maid?"

"Pretend not that yer doesn't take me meaning, Scallop," he said. "I'm here 'pon 'is Lordship's bizness, same as yerself."

Addison tried to hide that surprising news. He told him that he had not seen her in Florence and thought she might be lagging behind in Venice.

"Nay and nor will yer see 'her," Lobster Tail said. "She's a goner, that one. Should never have employed 'er, 'is Lordship R. I never did trust her a quarter farthing."

"Then she's skipped off. But to where?" Had the fumes in the shop and the late hour and day of travel made him so prone to shocks?

"Gone to 'er maker, for all I care." He took more wine.

"Nay, I'm pranking yer. Leif as not, she's run off with one of them Greek fellers that her Nibs and company befriended on the packet 'cross the channel." His little lower lip hair wavered, perhaps in slight mirth or worse, in an unconscious gesture Addison recalled from whenever he lied.

Addison realized two things with a shudder. First, that the pretty little French lady was dead. MacIlhenny had witnessed that death, if not caused it, to be so certain of it. And second, that she had also been in His Lordship's employ all the time he'd been following them.

He found this last most unsettling, suggesting as it did that Her Ladyship had been somehow induced to flee England, or at least, been very ably aided in doing so, although quite underhandedly, by *Lord R. himself*!

This did obviate Addison's own guilt in letting her escape him, although for what motive the Marchioness had been set up, Addison couldn't ascertain. He now wondered if he shouldn't have credited those gossips in Venice who spoke of Lord R.'s "being taken with that pottery heiress, Lady Georgiana Someone-or-other. Who'd recently been OBE'd by the Crown," his interlocutor from dinner had more said. "I understand she has pots of money, that Georgiana. Porcelain pots of it!"

Addison now suspected all this deliberate new information was carefully prepared exactly as Lobster Tail intended. Because, what if, in fact, he too had been following *Addison* all this time?

"She were me connexion, the little maid," Lobster said. "She left me notes to follow across two-thirds of the Continent. Like bread crumbs in a children's nursery tale."

Even more unsettling news. So, Lobster Tail *had* been following them.

"And now…?"

"And now, me fine lad Scallop, 'tis only yer and me to do it all. Just like old times, eh?"

He was exceptionally friendly, which Addison found most unsettling of all.

"Not only we two, Lobs. I have a man now in my employ."

"So I've seed. If the Tiger were here, she'd push out an older house-lad and install your lad in his own suite, like the one you had yerself. But I 'spect he's hardly good for anything more actively dire."

"Why? Does something more dire await us?"

"Well, 'is Lordship *do* wish something spercific accomplished," MacIlhenny said. "Spercific and soon."

"To snatch her up and bring her home? Isn't that the plan at this time?"

"P'raps! P'raps!"

He walked Addison back to his hotel, an arm over his shoulder, till Addison felt somewhat his prisoner. Lobster then joined the Italian lad and Addison as a tenant for the night there, sleeping upon the chaise in the outer chamber, as though on guard against any attempt to escape.

The following morning, Her Ladyship walked alongside her guard out of doors. Lobster Tail and Addison discussed taking her from him in a darkened alleyway where the two might overpower him while the third grasped her. They had decided on this course when Her Ladyship met up with some gentlemen, one evidently British or even American, two others Italian. As the odds were no longer in their favour, they were forced to desist.

That evening, those two men again joined the two of them. Again, they found no chance to accost her. Her Ladyship went indoors at nine of the clock and never came out that night.

Her Cerberus did come out, however, and they followed him across the bridge and river down to that place again. This time he entered, and they set about how to rid themselves of this nuisance.

Addison sent Luca in to enquire what the cost might be for a private room and also to get an idea of the spread of the place. Was it all separate chambers, or hastily constructed individual cabinets? Or was this a more promiscuous *fumitory* where imbibers of the drug would be placed bed next to bed? All in a row?

The latter, it proved, which was not best for their wants. But the chamber they might lease would be a semi-detached one, partly open to the *fumitory*.

Addison and Luca entered and secured that chamber. Lobster Tail was sent back to the hotel for stout rope and weapons he had purchased in a small railroad village two days before. Foreign mountaineers are common there, and such sales not at all remarkable.

Three Italian sisters operated this hellhole. They were tall, thin, shrewish-looking, and not to be charmed. Addison had Luca tell them he preferred not to smoke but merely witness, but this they would not abide. Addison must also purchase some of the stuff, smoke it or not. One of the establishment's already quite dissolute lads, still in his teens, showed Luca and Addison how to prepare the black, rubbery, pungent stuff for smoking and also how to prepare it to be drunk in a tiny cup of espresso. They thanked him and sent him on his way.

By the time Lobster Tail returned, Luca and Addison had separately circumnavigated the main floor and located their quarry. Addison believed he had seen him receive the opium and prepare it for himself in a small clay pipe. Like them, he was not placed out in the open among the hoi polloi—Addison thought him far too squeamish for that kind of promiscuity—but instead with a single wall parting him from the general area.

Because of the constant moving about and scrutinizing as the three woman and two lads tended to the needs of now this eater, now that smoker, they understood they must be extremely careful. Their movements must glide when at all visible, not be sudden or jerky. So, it was a long time before Addison could get himself over to the quarry's part-open chamber and secrete himself there. He'd set Luca apart as lookout and Lobster Tail between the two, as he might have to come to Addison's aid if the prey proved stronger than anticipated.

Lobster Tail held the ropes behind his waistcoat. All three men had sheathed *stiletti*, a sort of local poignard, sharply pointed and long enough to pierce anyone's heart.

The scene was unimaginably obscure, with the little lanterns by each bed dim and guttering when they weren't actually going out. The reflections upon the faces of the smokers, who lay in various contorted or log-like manners but who looked much like mere skeletons, even death's heads of men and women, was unsettling to a great degree. Luca was so frightened, he couldn't keep his eyes on any of them and thus he remained as lookout. Suddenly Addison heard the agreed-upon signal that none of the house ladies nor lads were in view, and a simultaneously a hand signal from Lobster Tail to go ahead.

Addison twisted himself out of the shadows and looked down upon the blackguard he had been following for so many weeks, the man he had come to regard as the Great Impediment to His Aim, and as the Blackest Fellow That Ever Existed.

He was not much older than Addison, spread supine on a torn and ratty sofa-chaise, all but lost to the world in his haze of opium smoke and fantastical dreams. His face was rapt, younger than ever Addison had seen it before. Even within the dim illumination from the rectangular bronze and mica lamps, Addison realized that he somehow *knew* him. Not from having followed him, but from some earlier, previous time or place. His coat and waist jacket had been removed and laid across a chair. His neck and chest were open to view, pale, smooth and soft. Ready for the stiletto.

Addison heard Lobster Tail whisper fiercely and saw him gesture to stab the fellow now that he was exposed. Addison had the stiletto in hand, and was ready to plunge it in, when the fellow turned, moaning softly and said in a low voice, "Nay, Father dear, thrash *me*! Not Tom! He is tender of years. Me, father, *me, Davey*!" Addison had heard these words before, many, many years ago, although he could at the moment not place where or when. Then he turned his face in his awful opium dream and his face settled out of his bad dream and into another.

Then Addison saw with astonishing clarity the half-moon scar on the drugged sleeper's lower cheek and chin!

Cicatrix Halb Mond, the starveling German hag predicted Addison would encounter weeks before in Aachen or Dortmund, his whore translating it as "a half moon scar," and Addison had scoffed at the words as so much trumpery. But here it was. Not only was it present, but Addison knew where it had come from: a broken ale-jar the boys' father had dropped. In his drunken stupor, he'd picked up a large piece and used it to attack the smaller of Addison's brothers. They two had hidden and whimpered behind the larger brother, himself only six years of age then, Addison's beloved elder brother, Davey.

Well did Addison recall the slice the drunken lout made in Davey's face, the gout and gush of boy blood, how the sot had stumbled backward, Davey's grunt of pain, the other boys' screams, their mother's terror when she ran in, the alarums she awakened in Villas Sheen, her rough binding up of Davey's face and neck, how he had been carried quickly to a medical student lodging near. Also, how Davey had shown up again some days later, sheepish, with a bright pink scar, this very scar before Addison! Their father had vanished for many weeks in fear of arrest.

"Davey!" Addison whispered, shaking his brother.

He half-woke in amazement to the name, and, seeing Addison, he was confused where and when he was.

"Davey! Brother mine! 'Tis I! Your little Addison. 'Tis I! Baby Addy!"

"Baby Addy!" He woke and sat up. "Baby Addy! Great stars! Alive! And well! Can it be so? How came you here?"

"First we must *go* from here!" Addison said. "Gather your belongings and I will help, for neither of us belong in this hellhole."

"You are the very reason I am here at all, brother, and why I have become an addict to fancies and dreams. To forget the past. To stanch my awful guilt. I cannot tell you for how many years I sought you or for how long I thought you dead and how long I thought myself to blame. Is it really you? Truly!" He put his hands over Addison's face and chest and Addison upon his chest, and they wept together.

When he looked up, Addison saw Lobster Tail whispering in a fury with Luca, who looked back in obvious fear. Addison went up to them. "We are mistaken. This is not who we thought it was. It is a grave error. This is a fellow near and dear to me. My very long-lost brother. Get you gone. I will see you at a later time."

Addison helped Davey dress himself for the street, and then guided and half carried him out of doors. One of the thin sisters remarked something in a disdainful voice as they exited.

The others were waiting and Addison told them it was a mistake. He sent them back to their hotel.

Lobster Tail went grumbling off at last, badly surprised

and not at all happy, for he had been looking forward to accomplishing dirty work that night, and Addison's discovery had thwarted him. As for Luca, he continued to lay about, as usual, a street or two distant from them for most of the hours of that long night.

A small private *ristorante* lay a street off, and Addison brought his brother there. He plied him with cups of *cafe espresso*, and he watched Davey awaken bit by bit, joyful to see his brother. Many a time that night, they stroked each other's dear, familiar faces and exchanged in broken sentences and half phrases their histories since they had last laid eyes upon each other.

Just as they were parting not long before sunrise, Davey said, "You do not know me well yet, young Addy. But if you did, you would understand I would not have taken on this close protection of a lady, unless I was well persuaded it was fully merited. And that her precipitous journey was necessary for her happiness and possibly for her very survival."

> October, 188—
> Albergo B—
> Florence, Italy

Sir,

As you will note, our journey in Your Service, following Her Ladyship has led us to this Italian city of great note, history, and outward beauty.

It has also led me to one of the Greatest Discoveries of My Life, and for this, I must thank you. It was the very greatest surprise of my own short and surprising existence, and one of the most important, upon which I believe you must agree, when at last I relate it.

Enough for now. Lest I burble on like a schoolgirl, I will tell it all in order.

Until that time when I may understand further all that pertains to this mission upon which I have been launched in your name, Lord, I am,
    Addison Grimmins Undershot

2. Post Scriptum

Davey, aka Stephen Undershot, had invited Addison to visit with himself and his charge in the little *palazzo* they were staying in. He made it clear she was awaiting a gentleman, whose aid had secured Davey's assistance. Until he arrived, Davey could not leave her for any period of time. "We have sustained a personal loss," she told Addison. "And though your dear brother tells me it was not substantial, still I held the little thing dear while I knew her." The Marchioness looked more relaxed than he'd seen her. She also looked younger. Was it the salubrious citrus and lavender scented air of Florence or merely freedom and a sense of impending safety?

"Your chambermaid?"

"Yes, you knew her?"

"Not at all."

"It turns out she was also in my…in Lord R.'s employ. As you were once, I understand."

"In England, yes."

"And now you stand with your brother staunchly?"

"Yes, I do."

"It's a miraculous discovery. And if no other good comes out of all this, your re-encountering after all these years surely will serve."

"There have been other benefits that have already come

out of all this," Addison's brother said. "What about your support and acquittal in that crisis of the two Greek brothers who were wrongly accused? Or how you helped that older woman who'd lost her jewels gambling."

"Yes. Yes. But enough!" She held up a hand. Addison recognized the pale grey gloves with little silver stitched holes above each knuckle, just as Crittenden, the cross-channel ferry purser, had described them. "Let's not spoil our luck by congratulating ourselves."

A servant of the owner came in to announce Mr. Henry James.

"A new but good friend, from Venice," she said to Addison. "Do you mind my meeting him alone? I know you both must have so much to say to each other."

Luca's gesticulations from the corridor meant he knew the new guest, and as they exited the room, he whispered to Addison. "That is the man in brown of whom I told you." He gestured toward his trouser front.

"Indeed. Stay near this room, Luca. If anyone tries to pass in—*not* from this house—call us immediately."

"Now in sun I see it," Luca said, looking from him to Davey and back before he left. "You two are brothers."

"We do have much to talk about," Addison said, once they were settled in the next parlour with tea before them. "You first, if you please."

Davey began. He well recalled bringing Addison from his mother's dying arms into that house and little school a few doors away. He had looked in on Addison later, when Addison was all unaware, and had rejoiced at his younger brother's good fortune in finding meat and affection, since he knew he could not himself keep him. Soon, their mother did indeed pass away, and Davey and Tom with only a single kind neighbour woman followed the one-horse dray with her body to a pauper's grave. Tom had gone to work in the pig market, and Davey sweeping the crossroads. They lived poorer than poor.

Once it was understood their father was gone for good, the boys were evicted from their lodging. Tom went to sea, just as Addison had been told when he first searched for him. There he'd been taken up or adopted by a sailor man who'd taken a fancy to him. All Davey knew was the fellow was known as James Wyatt, and the ship had sailed from Margate, but he didn't know its name nor its captain's name. Addison had not heard word nor tale of Tom for a decade after the news of him at sea, and he hoped he had flourished. At times he fancied Tom among South Pacific atolls and brown-skinned ladies he'd read about in half-shilling books.

But one time before he'd left off working for Tiger Jukes and was closer than before to the southern London docks, he heard two mariners talking about Lieutenant James Wyatt, and he'd closely queried them. If it was the same fellow, he'd been told, he'd certainly been lost with all hands in a commercial steamer during a giant of a tai-phoon somewhere off the Marquesas. Davey had also come upon that information, never confirmed, but he still declared himself happy for Tom, whose great wish had been to go to sea and to voyage widely and see the world's sights. He'd had over a decade of that life.

As for himself, Davey had joined the crew of sweeps of cross roads half times, and the other half at high house gutter cleaning and chimney sweeping. He might have grown and might have feebly prospered at both had not he one day given his one piece of corn-cake midday meal to his friend Charlie, who lay ill in a back alley, and needed it more. Weakened with hunger, Davey had that afternoon swept the crossroads as usual, but he'd gone faint and fallen in front of a passing carriage and almost been run down and run out of this life!

The chance that any Londoner would stop for a dazed lad was all but nil. The passenger of this vehicle, however, was a man from out of County Hampshire. Seeing the lad so ill-used and so poorly fed, he asked my brother's name and family and could barely make out through his own Christian pity and tears the answer, "None left, sir! All of them gone!"

He brought Davey to the townhouse he had taken in Poland Street and had him carried to bathe and then to bed, and he did not allow him up until the lad had the right colour in his cheeks and a mite of flesh upon his bones. That required three weeks' time, upon which Mr. Enos Walter Undershot Esq., his London business completed, quitted London-town, taking with him my brother Davey.

At Nine Oaks, the home Enos Walter shared with Delilah Jonathan, his widowed sister, Davey said he believed he had entered Eden. There he grew and prospered. He was tutored, fed, and taught to ride, fence, and sing.

There too, at Oldham, the town nearest to those lands, Davey was, at the age of eight years old, legally adopted by Mr. Enos Walter Undershot and soon made heir of his and his sister's all. He took the name of their beloved middle brother, killed in war abroad, Stephen Raglan Undershot.

Davey forgot much of his youthful past before that happiness, so dim, so dark, so full of foreboding and pain. He and his brothers always hungry and fearful, abandoned to poverty and violence. He revelled in being the son and heir of such generously high-spirited people, and he repaid them with love and many kindnesses.

Upon his twelfth birthday, the newly named Stephen joined his new father back in London-town, where his elder went again for business. He at last told Enos Walter that a younger brother existed, placed in good keeping with Mr. and Mrs. Gillip, and doubtless grown large, healthy, and wise by now—Addison.

Father and adopted son agreed to find the brother and perhaps take him for a day's drive into the country-side.

You may imagine then their shock and horror hearing Addison had been cast aside by those into whose care he had been so deeply entrusted. In vain, father and son searched the neighbouring streets and lanes, houses, and then hospitals and morgues for any word or sign. None was ever found but tantalizing hints: that a boy had sought Davey at the crossroads—by then, alas, gone, or that a lad had been to the great market seeking Tom, also by then gone. These traces had only made their search all the more agonizing. At last they concluded Addison had vanished into air or, more likely, passed into the earth itself. Perished. They must quit their useless quest and return to Hampshire.

So, now a serpent had entered Davey's Eden. Davey upbraided himself for not telling Enos of Addison's existence for so long and for not retrieving him sooner, for not saving his brother from the unreasoning wrath of his torturers. Although the truth was, Addison repeated, Davey could not have known of such things as they were occurring.

Outwardly, Davey was the very essence of a Walter Undershot son and nephew. How could he not be, they had been so kind? Inwardly, his torment never left him for a day. Whatever commercial newspapers fell into his hands, he perused for word of Addison. He haunted the lending library in Oldham for the same reason, and in coffee shops, he read those weekly gazettes of crime and scandal, searching for an unclaimed body. He imagined every horror come to his baby brother, and with every new horror he read of, he imagined Addison within its tentacled grip.

Soon, despite these secret fears, Stephen had become a young man, and he reached an understanding to wed a young woman of good family in the future. Still, his father and aunt both wished him to know something of the world before he retreated from it altogether. So it was that Enos Walter took Stephen abroad, first to France and Belgium, and then to Germany and Switzerland. Italy he took him to last, and Enos Walter was so ailing by that time they had to turn around rapidly; Undershot Sr. was quite ill indeed when they reached home at Nine Oaks at last.

There the old man quietly died of an evening, after dinner. His sister fretted and wished much company around herself after. Deeply grieving, Stephen wished no company. So, he went off to Heidelberg University where he was already enrolled, and he passed five long years abroad, writing back to Nine Oaks less and less frequently. He returned to witness his Aunt Delilah's illness, only to find the estate in the possession of strangers of her choosing, and his inheritance legally encumbered all about until he had attained the age of thirty years and, it was hoped, some semblance of maturity.

Nor was he surprised, for while in Germany he had allowed all his worst traits to come to fruition. He had gambled. He had drunk to excess. "Worse than our father, believe me, dearest Addison, how I regretted it!" He had duelled with rapiers, sabers, and even pistols, wounding but luckily never killing an opponent. All out of sheer rage at what he understood to be Addison's death and his uncaring part in it. In Prague, he found surcease from sorrows in that river of forgetfulness—opium. No doubt reports of all this had been made by one or another Englishman back to Nine Oaks.

Stephen returned, unchastened and unrepentant, to bury his Aunt Delilah and to in turn legally encumber all others but himself from retaining any part in Nine Oaks until he had attained the prescribed age. Only servants, faithful to him for the most part, would live there until he might legally return. And so, Stephen returned to London-town with a secured income and real prospects, but labouring when and where he would for periods of time as a Commercial Factor, buying and even sometimes selling portions of ship's cargos not otherwise accounted for to investors. Or as an investigator for one or another of his father's friends and business partners. He never failed the latter, but he also never allowed any of them intimacy nor closer looks into his life.

In time, the country lass he had once hope to affiance married another. The country friends died or retired. He found himself a free man, bound to none, responsible only to himself, but with a breadth of experience and knowledge of a man twice his age for all the wide variety of his sundry occupations. Among his acquaintance were by that time the highest to the lowest born.

It was as a man of the world, with a knowledge of Europe, that he had been approached by the friend of a friend of his long-dead stepfather's one afternoon at an office of law in Holborn. His mission was to go to Lancaster town and there meet with a lady. Once he had met her, his work had been outlined for him. He was to aid in her non-marital elopement from a manor, under the eyes of a hundred and twenty-five guests. He was to help her escape throughout Europe, and he was to place her into the hands of Her Friend, in Italy. The job would be of several months' duration and require all of his varied skills and abilities. The lady would undoubtedly be trailed, so he must deal daily with her potential captors.

So had two brothers found themselves at two very different ends of this affair.

❖

Addison walked across the street to meet with his brother in the *palazzo*. He'd had his bags sent over earlier and had only his hand-held travel *portmanteau* stuffed full and ready to come with him. He had sought in vain for Luca, who had vanished before he'd awakened. He hadn't seen McIlhenny since the aborted crime at the opium den the previous night. Addison hoped Luca had found a new position, or at the very least, those relations he claimed he had in Florence. If not, he would ask Luca to accompany him and Davey and "Mrs. Smith." And if he would not come, then Addison would return him to Venice with sufficient money. Of their third confederate, he did not know even where to begin to look. Lobster Tail came and went as though invisible at times. Perhaps he and Luca... But in the end, he was of no real importance.

Davey was outside the building when Addison arrived, and his and the lady's luggage and trunks were being placed around the back and top of a good-sized coach and four. They embraced again, and then went upstairs to get the lady. She was ready to leave and had said her goodbyes to the owners of her recent lodging. Addison picked up one of her smaller bags and Davey the other, and they went down those narrow stairs into the street. There stood Luca and MacIlhenny.

Addison spoke to Luca, making him understand by his better command of Italian and by gestures that he was welcome to come along and be a fourth in the coach. Luca agreed and went inside the *albergo* across the street to get his own smaller travel pack.

"And what of His Lordship's mission?" MacIlhenny said petulantly.

"I have written to His Lordship," Addison said. He flourished the letter in his hand.

"Saying what? That this one lives and that you are turned traitor?"

"What business is it of yours, Lobs? I hired you. Not His Lordship."

"So say you. He hired me in London. Sent me after you weeks ago."

"What do you mean?" Davey said.

"He knew to have the job done, he needed meself," MacIlhenny said, as they stood there in front of Her Ladyship's *palazzo*, awaiting her. Suddenly he unsheathed one of those Italian stilettos he kept and rushed at Davey.

Davey was able to step aside and received only a slash of his jacket sleeve and not even a cut to the arm, but Addison was incensed. He withdrew his own knife and the two went at each other. A small crowd quickly gathered, for these Italians liked nothing better than to see blood flow in the street, pushing Davey outside of their gathering so he could not interfere.

He rushed to the *albergo* to call for help. Luca leapt down the stairs three at time and they got to the street in time to push through and see Addison, who'd been holding his own in feints and jabs, stumble over some stone or kerb and fall backward.

MacIlhenny was upon him in a flash, stabbing him in the torso. Addison felt only pinpricks of pain but knew the next one could be fatal. He crossed his arms, presenting his forearms as targets.

His attacker swore at that but was suddenly pulled back almost up to his feet. Addison rolled away from the attack as quickly as he could and then began to feel the pain of the stab wounds as they spurted blood. When he next looked at the two, Luca had grabbed the fallen stiletto, pulled back MacIlhenny's head, and slashed at his throat so that blood gouted out upon Addison and the nearby onlookers.

Released, MacIlhenny grabbed at his throat and gurgled, reddened eyes staring at Addison as he stumbled to the ground only inches from him. The enraged Luca now plunged his stiletto into the Englishman's back once, twice, three times. *Oh my darling lad!*, Addison thought. *How good you are for me.*

"Come. Away with you!" Davey shouted and grabbed at Luca, pulled him out of the circle as if getting him free of the crowd and away from the *carabinieri*. *Oh, my darling brother. How clever you are for us.*

But his eyes were beginning to cloud over, and he wondered if indeed these would be his last thoughts ever, when suddenly the lady herself had dropped onto her knees before him. She was ripping out a section of her petticoat, using the cloth to stanch his wounds.

"*Medico! Pronto!*" She commanded the crowd like a queen. "*Aiuto! Pronto! Hai molto lire per lei a salvati!*"

"*Sono un medico,*" they both heard. A doctor was suddenly next to her. He was young and had a gorgeous moustache. Addison knew he was losing consciousness, but he wanted to kiss the fellow if only to feel that astonishing moustache against his lips.

Now women from her last residence were there with clean cloths, and the doctor had men lifting Addison and taking him up several steps and inside the cool darkness of the little *palazzo*. They were placing him on a divan, and the doctor was giving him something strong to smell under his nose and was asking him to move his eyes this way and that, and cutting off Addison's vest coat and shirt. He applied some kind of bandages, and now Davey was there.

"The lad is gotten to safety. But you! Oh, my Addison!" He wept. "We are so recently met. You must not leave me!" And he was taken away as Addison was lifted off the divan and tightly swaddled, and the doctor with the gorgeous moustache was saying something to the lady which sounded like he was to be watched all day and night. Addison could make that out very clearly. Then she was calming Davey, who seemed to be weeping inconsolably.

The lady was kneeling again by him. "You were heroic in defence of your brother, Mr. Grimmins. I see the black, withered hand of Lord R. has reached out many miles to do this deed. Only the most recent of many black deeds. But rest assured, no matter how you get on, and I'm am hoping for the best, your brother shall not be lacking sympathy, nor will he ever be lacking powerful friends in Italy."

Was he so very badly done in that they were all carrying on so, Addison had to wonder. He began to speak and she bent to listen, but all either heard were croaking sounds.

"Rest now," she said. "Be at rest. Here, drink at this," she said, holding a saucer with white powder in water. "You will explain it to me later on."

He sipped the liquid which he knew offered surcease of pain and, who knew, perhaps the surcease of all earthly sorrows as well. He managed to get out, "I...have...writ-ten pap—!"

"I will ensure that your brother gets your papers," she said very clearly and looked halo-ed, angelic, as she said so. "Never fear." Until about him it was all haloes now, no faces at all, and then...

3. Addison's Papers

The Writings of Addison Undershot aka Grimmins

Once, in the days of the Old Cavaliers, this befogged vicinity had been a sort of foreign traders' closed market. Not far away, a Synagogue squatted almost hidden behind its grimed walls. Both paid homage to some kind of Hebraic history of the place, and the squalid little demi-square our lodging looked out upon was known as Villas Sheen in honour of that past.

Like most of their ilk, my parents had wed young, and only after my mother had been "surprised with child." My father worked at odd jobs, never having a trade to speak of. Yet he was a tall and strong man and, when he was sober, he might well support a family of four. By the time I was born, he had a family of five, and he lost himself in labour much of the week and in gin the rest.

My mother was a good enough looking woman, or so I am told, cheerful, friendly, never a slattern. I recall her as an angel, naturally. But then, she died when I was less than five years old, so what could I know? She was not a drinker, yet she was unlearned and could never herself rise in fortune but must depend upon a man—and my sire saw to that only poorly. Four boys were born to them. Two lived, two died. I was fifth, and you know what they say of late children: loved the most or ignored the most.

By the time the two older were of schooling age, our father was more to be found unemployed than not, when he was to be found at all. For he had taken up, we'd heard, in another part of London, south of the River past Westminster, and we saw him seldom enough. As I dandled and nursed in what comfort I might take of my Ma, and as much affection as a child in such miserable condition could wish for, it was naught but toil for my siblings, albeit at not much pence per day.

The one swept the crossroads near Exchange Square, and the other was a clean-up lad, working amidst the pig butchery and suet rendering house at the Smithfield Mart. I recall them but vaguely and always as taciturn lads, their long hair scissored in front: closely so for the darker and elder one, to be neat for all the gents who might tip him at the Exchange Square, almost not cut at all for my second eldest and more ashen-haired sib, since it veiled him from the splash of hog blood and of swine guts.

He would come home and wash his face and hands very long minutes at a time at the open font out of doors before coming in, even in foul, freezing weather. Tom was his name. Davey was the other. I have no idea what has become of either lad, or if even they still live, since my destiny was soon to sweep me out of their ambit.

This happened when I was just half past four years old. My mother took a spring ague badly, and her unmarried older sister from six streets away was called on to take her care and mine too, which she did with a bad grace, brief though it was. Mother coughed and wheezed thereafter whenever the weather grew rank, which was nearly always, until she became too ailing to do more than feed me and see that I didn't harm myself.

I was told I was a tranquil infant who amused himself with whatever was at hand to become my toy and game. I seldom cried, and even when I was hungry rarely made an annoyance of myself. Unwell, unmedicated, penurious, alone, my mother took to her bed for extended hours. I was left alone until nightfall when my brothers returned home with a hot-pot of tavern soup and market leavings or whatever crusts they could cadge on Commercial Street.

As my mother grew weaker, 'twas a neighbour woman, Mrs. Gillip, who took me in more. She had a daughter named Susan whom she doted on, although she'd also doted on me since the time I was born, herself lacking any boy child. Though my Ma felt Mrs. Gillip had always wanted me for her own, and Ma tried not to let me go, what could she do? One morn, Davey carried me across the street to the Gillips' with what little toddler gear I possessed, and there stayed I, fed and dandled, and eventually taught my numbers and alphabet too, as it was a sort of school for infants.

Mrs Gillip prided herself upon her education on Brick Lane. And so Gillip's Nursery it was, formed on the model brought over from the Continent by the consort of Queen Victoria, called a *kinder-garten* or garden of little children. It was the talk of our northern vicinity of the city, I may well say. Clean and quiet, save for when Mrs. Gillip led us in singing. Every child washed hands and face several times per day and when coming in and leaving. Our food was healthy and without vermin—porridges and soups mostly, but with recognizable hunks of meat in the latter, a true rarity in the Villas Sheen.

No wonder other mothers got wind of it and left the little ones there for a day while their Mam went out buying a day's provender; or two days and nights running, while they visited family that resided outside the London Wall. Susan and myself stayed at Gillip's all the time, and we were paradigms of children: adorable to look at, unsoiled and cleanly clad, well fed, cheerful and intelligent. We were the smartest little things,

Susan with her banana curls and satin bows, me in my little sailor's suit and dickie.

Mrs. Regina Gillip was herself nothing to look upon. A pox had taken her early in life and had left its visiting card upon her face so that it was scarred from her pug nose on down. But her big blue eyes were as innocent as a china doll's. Her Harry Gillip doted upon her, and upon his very pretty Susan, who favoured her dam. After I had been there a bit, Harry even doted upon me too, as a new family member.

He worked at sundry occupations requiring a broad man with good shoulders and a deep voice. He'd worked the many boats that plied the docks at Southwark, and he had helped construct the new Thames river concrete and stone embankment that ran down from Strand to Westminster-town, and the newer bridges across the river, where I came to understand his booming voice was *de rigeur* for any construction team. His extensive back made him a rolled-sleeve model for several important painted pictures that were later on shown at French and English art salons.

Soon, more than a half dozen *kinder* might be found at supper and sleeping over nightly at the Nursery, with another half dozen day boarders. Mrs. Gillip had aspired to such; and she now dwelt in educational glory. I was all but a second child, second apple of Regina's eye, receiving as tasty morsels as Susan, as sweet a part of an apricot tart, a thick soup, and when Harry was flush, he brought home from the tavern a spicy East Indian stew, called a *Vindaloo*.

Paradise, alas, as our bard, Mr. Milton, shows us, is only recognizable when lost. I had resided in comfort and good vittles with the Gillips something like three years when my downfall occurred. Like that of our common ancestor, it was brought about through Woman. One of seven and a half years, and a flirt and grimalkin if ever one existed. Little Susan spread her feminine wiles about widely to each and every boy or man she came upon, sitting for a half hour upon dear Harry's lap, for example, fidgeting and fidgeting until she found a comfortable spot, upon which Harry would sigh aloud, put her down, and hurriedly leave the room. Still, I was her greatest attraction, partly because I saw her wiles for what they were. Even so, I couldn't help myself one late afternoon during our general laying down and mid-afternoon nap, but at her whispered urging followed her into the laundry corner.

Mrs. Gillip was sound asleep, snoring away from her labours. Susan then lifted her frock and said in a most seductive voice, "Show me what's in your pants."

"Same as you," I said, for I'd seen her make water in a pan once, even though she must bend down while I stood up.

"Silly. Silly. Silly! It's not the same."

I was taken aback. "It's not?"

"No, look!" said she and pulled down her pants just enough for me to look. Well! It was indeed quite different than mine or my brothers', and so I shook myself out of my flies to show her and she giggled. "See, silly!" Well, I saw, then she touched, then I touched, then she bussed my lips, and I bussed hers back, and it was in this very situation that Regina Gillip found us.

"Why! You! Fiend! You!" said Mrs. Gillip. Her face got almost purple, and I thought she might be taking a fit. Then she charged at us and grabbed me up, and before I could utter a word, she had thrashed me to pieces and tears. I'd never been touched in that fashion and was confused, wounded, and thoroughly out of sorts. When her arm had grown tired, she threw me down in a corner and covered me with old clothing. "Stay right there, filthy boy! Among the filthy clothes. And don't you dare move an inch!" She then took up Susan, but rather than thrash her as she done me, she cooed at her, and kissed and caressed her and asked was she unhurt and fed her a sweetmeat and then brought her out to the other *kinder*, who had been awakened by the noise she'd made beating me.

 I remained hidden under old clothing all that afternoon, and had no tea and bread and butter. Once when I crawled out to look at what treats the others were eating, one boy saw me, and Regina Gillip saw him see me and she leapt up and chased me back into the corner and under the old unwashed clothing, kicking at me.

 The day the boarders left, Harry returned home and I heard him taken aside and told of my sin. "The blackguard!" he yelped. "The whelping little cur. Shall I thrash him again?" But I was not thrashed again. Instead, I was left to remain where I was by Mrs. Gillip after she had fed and put the other children to sleep, and there I lay, hungry, and cold, wrapping soiled petticoats about me for warmth, utterly unclear as to my offence.

 The next day I was allowed out to wash up and join the others. But Mrs. Gillip pretended I was not in the house. I received no food, and when I tried to sleep, no place was left for me and I had to go back into the laundry corner. The same went for the afternoon and night. I was ravenous, and after the others had gone to bed, I got up and sneaked to the cold larder and there fed myself on what crusts were left over.

 I might have gone on like that for weeks more had I not been caught by Mrs. Gillip. She thrashed me again and the very next morning, Harry grabbed me up like old laundry before I could even open my eyes for the day, and carried out by my middle like a dead fowl. After he had strode near on a mile without saying a word or heeding my pleas, I was dropped onto the cobblestones and next to me was tossed a tied-up bundle of the clothes that I had arrived in some years before. Before I could gather my wits, he was striding off into the fog, and it was not yet seven of the morning.

I cowered cold in a corner as the day began, and then that shop door was opened and I was kicked aside. I begged and got a half-eaten brown bread roll. Soon enough, some toughs twice my age arrived and announced that this was "their kingdom" and if I knew what was good for me, I would "establish myself elsewhere."

I asked a passing charwoman what that large building was and was told it was St. Bartholomew's Hospital. I recalled my brother Davey saying it was near the Smithfield Market where brother Tom worked. So I dragged myself through Smithfield Circle, with its grim statue of Henry the Wife Killer, until I found the market.

So immense it was, I was lost on an instant. But then I recalled it was hog butchery my brother Tom worked at, and so little by little, I worked my way to that end. Once found, I went into every shop and asked for Tom. But there was none of that name, and the blood-splattered boys and men all seemed listless as they answered me no. I'd just given up hope when one of the oldest men there with a great beard pointed like a spade, came to me and said, "Is it little blond Tom with the long hair you're looking for?"

"Yes, from Villas Sheen in Bell's Lane?" I said.

He shook his head a while and then described him well enough, concluding, "Gone."

"Gone, sir?"

"Gone to sea, the boy is. Over a fortnight. He laboured for me."

"To sea?" It was as good as Tom having died and gone off to heaven.

I was at least able to get directions to Exchange Square

and slowly wended my way back east into the city, whence I'd been hauled that morning. There I sought my brother Davey among the sweeping boys. But he was not to be found, and when I asked the sweepers they said he got a real job working for a gentleman far outside the city, beyond Westminster in the country somewhere.

One boy asked if I'd eaten and kindly shared a small two-day-old meat pie with me. For Davey's sake, I supposed. Looking at my bundle, he asked what they were, and when I showed them, he said he could take me to a shop where I might sell the clothing for money. I got sixpence for the pretty but now useless things. I bought another meat pie and then, since I was almost there, I walked dejectedly back to White's Row.

The woman who lived in front of us at Villas Sheen recalled me, and she marvelled at how tall and well I had grown. Of my brothers she said, "Once yer Mam was dead, they wuz trown bodily from the rooms. Poor lads. Slept under the street bridges or in constriction of the rail termeenuss, or so I gaither." She fed me soup, but there was not even space on the floor for me to huddle, and so I left.

The few street bridges I found were already filled with children and men jostling for a place to sleep. She had given me a ragged half-blanket, and I wandered about in a trance of sorts, despondent at my destiny, until it was very long past midnight.

I was about to fall down right there in some doorway to sleep when I spotted a few boys hurrying in a particular direction. I followed them to the Bishopsgate Railway Terminus. Adjacent to it, via a little wooden doorway, turned out to be an enormous construction site, of what would in a year or more become the Liverpool Station, the grandest in all England. There, the boys entered, then slid under some wooden hoddings and were quickly out of sight. I followed and entered into a Herculean excavation.

I saw the lads headed toward one particular area, and I followed them to where the building of what would be the lowest portions of the new railway terminus was already in progress. Of course there was a night watchman and a dog, but they were old and half deaf. Anyway, the place was gigantic, bigger than all of London, I thought, I who had seen so little of it. So, I did what I saw other young boys doing. I climbed up until I was on a high rafter, out of sight of watchmen and dogs, and then I wedged myself into a wall space where I slept.

That night and a week more nights. All the while spending money on pies and bread rolls, the cheapest food I might get, asking if anyone knew Davey or Tom. But there were so many Daveys and Toms and I had only their Christian names.

Soon my food and money gave out, and it was then I remembered seeing a little knot of the dirtiest boys all gathered about in one portion of the terminus site which was that best covered with canvas against the weather. These were called by the others Grimmins Lads. Unlike the other boys and men who scattered like so many black beetles at the approach of dawn, these lads remained as they were, in a group of ten. They were met at morn by an open-backed, horse-drawn dray which took them away and brought them back there to sleep after nightfall. Unlike the rest of us, too, they were a compact and unified group, staunchly defending their little territory and sharing drink and vittles amongst themselves and even lighting a fire for warmth. How they had treasoned the watchman and dog I never found out. Those guardians never went near them.

One morning as they gathered where they were used to meeting the dray, hunger sparked me to dare approach them, and I asked if they were going to work.

Two of them my age looked me up and down slowly, and one said, "Dustbins!"

Before I could utter more than, "Might I come work there too at Dustbins?" we heard the clopping of a well-shod horse. They all clambered up into the open back of it behind the driver.

He turned round, seeing me standing there, and said, "What's this then?"

"He wants to come," said one of the boys I had been talking to.

"Dustbins," said I, not knowing what I was saying, thinking perhaps that it was a place of especial manufacture.

"Well, then, let's take a look." He leapt off and came down to look me over. If the boys were the dirtiest I'd ever seen, he was the very cleanest man. He was tall, and not yet forty years of age, with yellow hair which shone as though newly washed. His face and neck were pale yet not quite pink, and so astoundingly clear they had a sort of glow. His jacket and coat were simple, his trousers equally so, but immaculately unsoiled. His gloves, albeit ecru, were the most unspotted I had ever laid eyes on. Coming up to me, he spun me about like a top, then pulled up my lip as one does a horse. He felt of my arms and legs. All the time making little comments. Of the teeth, "Straight!" Of the arms, "not fat," and of the legs, "strong."

"I need employment, sir."

"Do you now? But does employment need you? Does…" He paused for dramatic effect and stared me down. "Does the *Dustbins* need you, you young Scallop?" He looked back at the boys gathered to watch. "Crayfish, how much did you earn last year?"

"Six quid to keep for myself," the filthy boy said.

"Lobster Tail? You?"

"Seven and six."

"Prawn?"

"Nine and three."

"Nine and three!" the man remarked with a little whistle. "Now that's employment, my little Scallop, for you are tarty looking like a lower Thames scallop, isn't he, Oyster?"

"Fat as an oyster," replied little Oyster.

"We labour six days and rest the Sabbath," this very clean man said. "The sixth day is your earning. All the rest, you labour for me. For this labour, you shall receive ale, pies, broth, bread and tarts and stews. Is this satisfactory, my young Scallop?"

"It's satisfactory."

"Good! I am Andrew Marvell Grimmins, yes, yes, named after the great poet. You from henceforth are Scallop. And you are henceforth a Grimmins Lad. Welcome him, all." And so doing, he lifted me with one hand and tossed me atop the others. I tumbled and was pinched and pummelled in welcome by three or four lads. And soon enough our free-for-all was made even more chaotic when Grimmins got on the driver's shelf and started up the dray. Then we had to hold on to either side as she bucked and cavorted.

❖

I've mentioned I'd seen very little of London-town. Indeed, the previous day's sordid and difficult journey was the greatest amount of travel I'd ever done in my short life. You may imagine then how, once all the jostling was at last done with, how I sat and gaped almost open-mouthed at all about me.

"Catching flies, is he?" said Lobster Tail and shut my mouth for me.

The dray headed directly south along Bishopsgate, crossing Threadneedle Street then Cornhill Street and suddenly becoming a new thoroughfare called Grace Church Street, surrounded by much older structures. To our left was Leadenhall Market, "a cinch to pinch," according to Prawn, though what he meant I only would come to know later.

There ahead of us was the oldest part of the city, with Eastcheap Street's many shops, and the enormous monument sitting there on its own little island amidst all the dray, cab, hackney, omnibus, landau, closed-coach, horse, and pedestrian traffic. Soon we had attained King William Street, and there in the distance lay the amazing, the stupefying, the astonishing London Bridge and Tower themselves. I'd heard and read of them often enough in my *Kindergarten Reader*. We swung suddenly left onto Lower Thames Street. Events happened too quickly for me to make them out or follow the other boys' words, and what follows is more a reconstruction from many such rides over many more months, allowing me to point out the enormous and greatly pungent Billingsgate Fish Market, and the equally elderly Customs House, put up by Sir Christopher Wren, that bird of beauty.

Our way lay just beyond those contrasting edifices: one slapdash and seething with life, the older starched and reticent. And there, in a tiny *cul de sac* with only a few multi-levelled house fronts, lay what would become the new centre of my life. The dray stopped, and A.M. Grimmins slid off his driver's box, but not before checking the rutted street below for traces of ordure and dirty water. As he got down, he undid the whitest handkerchief I'd ever laid eyes on and wiped the driver's seat, then covered it over with sort of a canvas tarpaulin.

By now his Lads were fallen or leapt or pushed out of the dray, tumbling about and swotting each other before the middle and most dilapidated of three doorways that appeared to all lean in toward each other.

The Lads made way for Grimmins, who wiped off a substantial key before and after fitting it to the boy's eye-high lock. He stepped quickly away as the lads stumbled, tumbled, leap-frogged, and otherwise gambolled in through the narrow dark hallway. I had held back, and A.M. Grimmins now swanned a languid hand, bidding me enter. I could feel him darken the doorway and shut and lock it behind me.

From the moment I'd heard the word "Dustbins," I'd developed certain preconceptions of what I might discover. First, and most foremost, I expected to encounter a mile of dust, dirt, and garbage. It would make great sense given the boys were so utterly unwashed. Secondly, I'd presupposed it was a sobriquet for a particularly dusty and or dirty manufactory of some unknown household object.

What I beheld was a five-storey-high, partly ceilinged, glass-windowed mountain of refuse. Well, official and domestic debris is more accurate. In the early morning sunlight, the cyclopean, irregular, vast mounds sparkled and glittered. And it was that very sparkle that we lads were most after. For this huge collection of locally residential, Court, and commercial wastage was dropped here untouched, unsorted, unlooked at by those who amassed it from out of back alley, side street, below street, and stable side refuse cannisters.

Separated from the organic ilk of filth—for the greater part—it was primarily and overpoweringly dry. So dry, that within hours I would be sniffling. In a few more hours, my nose would suddenly erupt in rivulets of red blood to the cheers of whatever other Lads were nearby. "Look at 'im. 'E's got a gusher," Dungeness cried in delight.

Secondarily, and this is connected with the first, the waste was essentially composed of paper products even though it was predominantly dove to dark grey *en masse*, not white like most of the paper itself. Thirdly, and most importantly, it was unsorted. Sorting or sifting through it was to be our own lovely work, for which our hands must have gloves of a sort. One of our elders, Crustacean, tossed me a series of cloth rag strips and displayed for me upon his filthy digits how to wrap them about my hands and tuck them in. "Be a mass of bloody 'ands he'd be without 'em rags." Crustacean sniggered at the for him evidently happy thought.

Each of us had our own unique territory within that Herculean accumulation: mine own was known as Lesser Byward, as it seemed to point in the general direction of that external lane. Of course this was, by the Lads' standards, one of the more inferior locales. The latter being evaluated by the criteria of how much "acteral swag," according to Crustacean, was once or might be consistently obtained from any particular vicinity. As the pile-up varied from day to day, this seemed like purest mythology to me, but Lads had been known to break each other's noses in arguments over someone else taking their "cherce lanes."

I soon discovered after we entered and had been fed day-old sweet rolls and a small pot of ale with a little fizz remaining it—my first alcohol—that our work was to enter our "lanes" with a sort of swimming motion, hoping to dislodge, disturb, and otherwise loosen up that mountain of debris a bit, but not too much. Once inside, which is to say some three to four feet deep, we were to begin picking through and locating treasure. We each wore a cloth bag across our front, much like a grocer's apron, in which to place the swag until it could be sorted more carefully.

As with any apprenticeship to any craft, no matter how peculiar or arcane, there were overriding rules as well as well-proven taboos. One should not ever go so deep or so low into one's lane that one risked being trapped by a "fall over" or, even worse, a "cave-in." Such had once happened to poor little Sea Urchin, who had since that day never been located again. Vague rustlings and ever fainter cries for help lasting nearly another week had been heard following his disappearance down, down, deeply down into his lane, but the lad himself was never seen alive again and at last was given up for lost, his name a warning to all—or at least to me, as in, "Don't be an Urchin, eh, there, Scallop!"

As bad or worse a destiny was "holding back" on one of Andrew Marvell Grimmins's five days. What one did on one's own day mattered not. But that very clean man could become, I was assured by each and sundry boy, a veritable "demon outta very hell," according to Little Tarpon, who had witnessed one such ill-judged holding back of a discarded paste jewel tiara by one unfortunate boy, Ocean Anemone.

"Thrashed?" asked I, who'd only recently found out such a thing was possible in life.

"Near skinned alive. If Lobs and me hadn't run inbertwixt him and Nemo, he'd have no rear left to ever be caned agin, never mind sit 'pon."

The fate of poor Ocean Anemone was a cautionary tale for us all. He'd been thrashed and then exiled out the front door of the Dustbins Paradise. Forbidden to ever again to re-enter those holy gates, Anemone supposedly languished outside long enough to be seen and then dragged inside the next tall edifice by a very tall, elderly old maid, who—and this was said with such horror it took me a while to make out—*bathed* the boy repeatedly and so assiduously that he was rendered unrecognizable.

"'Ereafter, 'e smelled like a flaking roose." Tarpon wrinkled his nose in disgust at his fellow boy's heartrending fate. "Schooled to this day, indoors and out. Wears a cravat." And then, the most crushing condemnation of all from any true Grimmins Lad. "'E carries nothing greater in his pocket than a ha'pence!" sneered Lobster Tail.

I, of course, would have spun cartwheels upon my head to have had a ha'pence in my pocket. Even so, I heeded my elders and betters and was carefully instructed to keep my wits about me and to be constantly on the lookout for any such sinister spinsters exhibiting sanitary schemes or educational designs upon my innocent self.

The first day, I shared Little Tarpon's lane, he being the slimmest and lightest of weight, and he showed me how to obtain treasures out of the great heap of waste, which contained so many brightly false leads. In this manner did I quickly learn that sealing wax was of great use. One pulled out a letter, and if it was waxed, as many official papers were, one determined by fingering it how thick the wax was. If of a certain thickness, it was valuable and might be scraped off and re-moulded into tapers, and Andrew Marvell Grimmins or one of his Lads profit thereby.

Any metal whatever was to be retrieved, whether it be partial, scrap, sliver or whole. From chamber pot to pen squib to ale tankard, it could be profitable. Similarly, any crockery or pottery, from porcelain down to grub-stone, was to be gathered. Fur, cloth, leather, quill, pencil-lead, and any and all wood larger beyond a splinter was to be taken, too.

It soon became astonishingly remarkable to me what folk discarded. Toy boats with half masts and parchment sails; paste pots still one quarter filled with glop; copper finger-rings missing only their inset stone; candle ends; foxed notebooks; girdled book spines without boards; pen nibs by the hundred-fold; rancid lamp oil, including a half litre of once quite redolent spermaceti; scrimshaw and uncarved ivory combs and knitting needles; canvas and other heavy sail cloths; wooden boxes of all sizes; unused stationery paper of the thickest, softest weave and finish; little blackened metal tubs still holding a smudge of ink; iron nails, bent or straight; brass door fixtures, tarnished or not; sheared-off crystal paperweights; teak and ebony wooden back teeth; half-wigs and demi-perukes, especially those days when the Holborn Courts dust-drays delivered to us; hair dye in little cyan bottles; carpet ends; and bent-to-be-woven basket osiers.

Whenever we found triangle papers of unknown pharmaceuticals, we invariably licked them off and gulped them down, usually putting on a great show of swooning, in pretence of a reaction. One time, I came upon a complete seven inch long *Copp-a-cola*, a savoury dried meat the breadth of my arm and far tastier that we Lads shared late that night, Grimmins having thrown it to us, more concerned as he was with the very fine, blue and gold metal foil it had come wrapped inside. It had found its way to us from an Italian city I read from that hurriedly snatched label—Parma. Perhaps I shall be there myself soon.

Naturally, I returned to the construction site after we had feasted every night, our supper being of whatever unspoiled and unrancid foodstuffs any of had come upon that day, in addition to regular portions of small, yeasty meat pies and enough ale to get the younger of us sleepy, all of it ordered by Grimmins at a bulk rate from a local tavern known as the Deaf Hound. If Grimmins was in a good temper, we might also divide a gooseberry or pear tart that his landlady, who was said by the elder Lads to be wooing him, had baked. That would sweeten our palates.

That first night I slept in surprising comfort and warmth, exhausted, surrounded and yet not overly bothered by the rank aromas of many dirty boys. By the second evening and onward, I would fall to sleep instantly and awaken in an hour or so to hear one or two of the older Lads telling stories, but I would quickly fall asleep again.

Within a week, I had made the first find I might keep myself—a particularly handsome green marble lamp base, cracked neatly in half and ringed in brass—that Grimmins then bought off me for a quid. That was more money than I'd ever seen, and I would stare at the large fat, somewhat chewed-edge coin with growing pleasure, thinking what tasties and pasties it would buy.

A week later, I realized I had become a Grimmins Lad in yet another way. We had no employment Sunday afternoons, A.M. Grimmins's only acknowledgement of the existence of a power higher, or cleaner, than himself. Left to our own devices after morning labours, we would remain at Thameside on all but the rainiest of days, and there too we naturally rushed through Billingsgate Market for what Prawn referred to as "loose change," i.e., anything whatsoever of value not tied down or pushed deep in someone's pockets. At the nearby Swan Lane Pier, in those years, a sort of impromptu fish-fry caravan was invariably lodged for several hours midday. It belonged to two fat and rather jolly sisters, the Cridleys, who for a very few ha'pence would well feed a bundle of dirty Lads, so long as we remained out of sight of the 'van's more respectable clientele.

It was on one such Sunday near sunset when we had feasted well, thanks to Evangelina and Leona Cridley's generosity with our few offered ha'pence, that we began tumbling about swotting each other and somehow or other myself and Crustacean found ourselves rolling further on and crossing paths with a brace of somewhat down at heels clergy who'd also just finished their repast in front of the 'van.

"You are the filthiest children I ever laid eyes upon," said one demi-divine, with hair so yellow it looked green, while the other spat upon the ground.

"Undesired bastards," he said.

We immediately made fun of the two, but later on that day, I found myself thinking, he couldn't have meant me, could he?

Those half free days, we used to beg at the open common in front of the Tower by the statue called Hammer Thrower, in truth more for hilarity than for pelf, and as we passed a horse trough an hour after, I stared into the reflection of its unstirred waters. I was indeed grimy. In weeks to come, I would look into another trough or shop window and so my progress in dirtiness as a Grimmins Lad was made inexorably clear. I advanced from grimy to grubby, thence to grungy, from smoky to dusty, until I had achieved the ultimate and was truly sooty in hue.

Like the other Lads, I would pick up whatever bits of cloth or ornamentation Grimmins disdained, employing them to spottily embellish my increasingly dirty clothing. None of us actually looked poor, tattered, or ragged. We thought that we resembled ocean-going pirates and as yet unhung highwaymen. Later on, I would realised we looked childishly outlandish.

One other Sunday when some of us were "taking the air," as Prawn put it, sticking out his rump and head in different directions as though he were a fat lady with a bustle, at Tower Pier, a laughing young woman walking with a group of young people came up to me.

She held her handkerchief in front of her face and said, "You are aware, young man, that the brooch upon your breast contains a precious stone?"

I had found the brooch the day before, on one of my own days, but I hadn't yet shown it to Grimmins, who had been otherwise occupied, and I was so surprised by the encounter that I replied, "No 'tisn't . Anyway, I found it in a dustbin," so she would know I'd not stolen it.

"Then you are fortunate indeed, although your appearance suggests you actually rendezvous in dustbins a great deal," she said with good humour. "The stone is real. It's called a beryl. And that one looks to weigh five or six carats."

"Would you like it, Miss?" I offered to remove it.

She laughed. "I don't have enough money to pay you for it, and as I am a proper young lady, I may not accept a gift from a stranger," said she, then moved away.

"Is it worth a quid, then?" I asked, since that was the amount Grimmins commonly offered us for such sparkling finds.

"Five guineas at least," said she, turning around to whisper it.

I immediately unpinned it from my chest, wrapped it in cloth, and hid it upon my person. This act would prove crucially serviceable in later days, and I would thank that young lady for it.

I've mentioned I would sometimes awaken and hear some of the older Lads telling stories. One evening, something that one of them, Lobster Tail it was, said caught my attention, and I quietly swotted myself awake to listen.

"Two and fourpence she said it was worth? He only gave a quid for it?"

"He offered a quid 'nd a hav!"

"Just as bad. Did you face 'im wid it?"

"So's I did. I said, 'Miz Cridley ov the 'vans wants it an she'll pay better.' I told 'im how much and 'e sez, 'She's a fool then, that one. Take it, me Lad,' and 'e tost it at me. But yer could tell Old A.M. rued letting it go."

"An easy way out. But I take yer point, old Lobs."

"Do yer, Crusty?"

"Aye, and I advise yer to no more nivir agen tells him such as that. 'Tiz how poor Starfish met 'is own end."

"Starfish?"

"Afore yer time, Lobs. The best of the best of we Lads, and the best earner and finder ov all. He found out one time a copper and bone pen set was worth a quid or more and was offered two shillings on it and ack-ooosed the Big Feller ov theevery. Steeling from pooer hapless youths, said he."

"Aye. And what wer his comeuppance?" Lobster Tail asked.

"Don' know. Nivir saw the Lad agen. Up and vanished, he did, with nary a word to none of we."

The two of them made a similar humming sound.

"'Nd so, Lobs, I advise yer agen to nivir agen tell him nothing like that."

"Starfish was in his rights, then?"

"De yer want ter be a Lad? De yer want ter have a roof to sleep oonder and ale and meat pies? Iv yer do, them's the unspoke rooles."

"So's if'n I find sum'ing valerble, I keeps it? I donts offer it him?"

"Yer said it, Lobs. Not me. G'night."

The very next afternoon, when we was tumbling about during one of our several impromptu free time periods, Crustacean grabbed me especially hard and very quietly said to me, "Keeps what yer heard las' nigh' ter yerself, hear?" and accented his comment with a twist of my ear.

It wasn't difficult to elude the other Lads when I needed to, and so I got my precious beryl to Evangelina Cridley, who looked at it—holding her nose—and said, "Too rich for my blood, laddie. Yer'll need to go to Mr. Hausfroth fer that."

We'd passed the Hausfroth Antiquities shop on a few occasions, so I asked, "Will he let me in the door, then?"

When she made a moue with her magenta painted lips, I added, "Pr'aps for a gift, you'd do it for me, Miss Cridley?" We settled on a twenty percent cut for her, and I asked her to give me a receipt, which she did, most surprised I could read.

"His Nibs don't know you can read, do he? 'Causing if he did!" she warned. When I looked surprised, she said, "He must keep account books of some sort, showing his earnings *above* his payment for the Lads' finds." Which meant she and her sister had suspected his theft all along.

Suddenly I understood. Even so, discretion—as my little *Alphabetical Reader* at the Gillips Kindergarten had taught me—is the better part of valour, and I waited until she had gone to Hausfroth and brought me back the royal amount of four pounds, nine shillings and sixpence *after* her percentage was taken, which I then secreted upon my person in various areas by loopings and threads, before I decided to see exactly how much the very clean Mr. Grimmins profited off his Lads.

Weeks would pass before I had my chance, but it came. Grimmins was called out by a "client" to adjudge some largish amount of what he claimed was "frippery." Crustacean was put in charge of the Lads, and as I continually asked for the smaller piles of waste, closest to Grimmins's office in just such an event, he was easy enough to circumvent.

Within the office, the account books were findable. But only just, and after some fooling about searching with the greatest of care, one ear turned all the while to the doorway. At last, two tooled leather sheafs were unshelved that produced results. One was titled *His Garden* the other *His Coy Mistress*. Only later on would I discover these were references to the poet Marvell's works. But one ledger clearly showed Grimmins's payment to us, and the other ledger his sale of the varied items. And at what—usually far greater—profit.

The books could not be removed without him noticing,

so I had to find a way to get my way into the office and copy them.

Again, it was a matter of selecting poor dustbin finding locations near his office and waiting until Lobster Tail or Prawn or whomever he put watch over us was away. And it also meant sacrificing some of my own day's findings to Grimmins to allay suspicions that I was not working my share for him on "his" days.

Months went by in this matter. I had passed my eighth birthday and was quickly approaching my ninth when I finally had it all in hand.

Now, to do it carefully. Crustacean and Dungeness were the best finders, and consequently the two most often and most thoroughly stolen from, so they must be approached first. I got them together on a ruse during one Tower Sunday afternoon outing, and told them the facts. I then read them what their finds had actually earned to Grimmins, compared to what they were paid for them.

They were as astonished by my reading skills as by the thoroughness of the theft perpetrated upon them, but still I needed proof, and the Cridley sisters provided that. The word spread that night, and once we were all back in our construction site sleeping den, a sort of general council of all the Lads was held. There I read aloud each boy's finds and Grimmins's most obscene profiting off it. Lobster Tail, the oldest, one of the least sinned against since Grimmins paid more the older and wiser you got—but also the most conservative of the Lads, cautioned us and enjoined silence and patience. But Crustacean and others were far more vexed and wanted blood.

A compromise plan of sorts was at last worked out. The next day was Monday, and several of the elder boys would draw Grimmins away from the office. I would then go get the two ledgers and hide them. When he realized they were gone, we were to deny to a Lad knowing anything. I would then begin dropping single sheets of the copies I had made of his accounts from the ledgers upon the path between the outer door and his office. This would enlighten him to what exactly was known, as well as who knew it.

I'm not exactly certain what we expected. All the Lads save myself and maybe Crustacean wished to continue to do business unmolested with A.M. Grimmins, revealed crook though he may be, because that was what we knew and what we did for our living. Somehow, there was a general belief he would laugh, recognize that he was caught, and immediately change his ways. And we would all go on as before, except that he would now pay us properly. Did I mention that we were all boys between the ages of six and twelve?

Anyway, that was how our plan began to manifest. *Began.* For it quickly became clear to a few of us that in addition to extreme cleanliness, A.M. Grimmins also displayed to a fault that other Christian virtue, extreme guilt. Once the account papers copies were dropped, he became as a hunted animal. He darted out of his office every few minutes. He became nervous and looked about himself all the time. He was brief with us to the point of enigmatic laconity. Still, a page floated in front of his office door. He exited—we posted a spy to report it—snatched it up before anyone else could see it, and darted back into his office.

Next day a new tactic: nailing the account pages to his office door. And when this also failed to bring about the result we sought, nailing it to the door of the outside loo. According to Little Tarpon, whose "line" that day was closest to the office, Grimmins emerged from what had evidently been a particularly satisfactory bout of defecation only to see the account copy on the loo door and he began screaming, then screeching, all but foaming at the mouth.

When Little Tarp stepped forward to impel some admission from Grimmins, the cleanest man in London grabbed him about the throat and began to strangle him. We had to beat A.M. off the boy with sticks and whatever other implements were to hand.

He let go of Tarpon and turned to face his Lads, his creations, after all. He was all but snarling. "Who?" he demanded. "Who is putting those up?"

"I am," said I, standing forward.

"I am," said Crustacean.

"Me too," said Lobster Tail, until it was clear we all knew what was going on, and all the Lads came forward.

Grimmins looked at us as though we were he-devils from Hades.

"No," Grimmins said, and we didn't have to ask what he was referring to as he repeated it. "No," meant he would not capitulate.

"If no, then," said Lobster Tail, our leader, "we go. We go and we warn any other lad from coming here ever again. End of the business."

"Noooooooo!" Grimmins howled. "Noooooooooooooo!"

In his voice was all the persecuted perplexity of a wounded wild creature caught in a man-trap.

"There is another way," said I.

"How it will happen from now on, is that one of us," Lobster Tail went on, "will account *alongside* yerself."

This was an even more intolerable future, and Grimmins was all but frothing at the mouth until he realized what Lobs had said.

"Which one of you?"

I knew this was a trap to catch me out, and I immediately countered it. "We shall take turns."

"Nooooooooooooooooooo!" Grimmins saw no possible

way of saving face now, and he began charging first at me, blocked by two boys, then at Lobster, blocked by two more, then at Crustacean. He headed for Little Tarpon but dashed right past him and out of our circle.

We watched him in great amazement as he rushed toward the highest and most unsteady of the newly arrived dust piles. He simply bolted up its side, scrambling and tumbling about like a set-on-fire alley cat.

Where did he think he was going? Or was he even thinking by then?

Grimmins had obtained some thirty yards' height before he stopped running, perhaps realizing exactly where it was that he had run to. He hung there a longish while, before his weight was suddenly felt. We first saw him shift position as though to get a bit more comfortable, before his hands went down on either side as though he were grasping at security. There was no security, however. Only seventy feet of loose paper, and he simply dropped out of view.

Driven by our own fear, we all rushed helter-skelter up the dust pile and sought to find him by brushing aside various sub-lines to peer into the depths. At last, Prawn found one such line going deep, and we could just make out the very top of Grimmins's well shampooed and beautifully combed-over head, a mere dot very far away in the depths of the dust pile below. Then he raised up his hands, his beautiful, clean hands, now covered with filth and stained by ink before that line and all around it collapsed into itself, and we had to quickly scramble to get away or else also fall into the morass below.

After about an hour of stunned silence, it was made clear Andrew Marvell Grimmins was buried over forever. Crustacean and I located the office safe box and managed to get it open, but there was no more than twenty pounds inside, mostly in smaller change. We distributed it equally until it was all gone. That night, Lobster Tail sat on the dray's box, took up the reins, and drove us to the construction site. We ate better than usual that evening and slept at our usual spots, but very next morning, we all knew we must go our own ways. Just at dawn, Prawn awakened me.

"We're off, then."

"Where to?" I asked.

"Who knows?"

I slept in until roused by the construction workmen's hammers. Then I gathered myself up, with my total Dustbin earnings from a year and a half plus the final distribution, totalling fifteen pounds. I located myself a horse fountain spigot and hose and washed myself as clean as I could get before I was chased off the construction site. The next nine months, I would lounge about London, travelling, seeing the sights, and enjoying life.

So did the other Lads. At least those who didn't all spend their pelf on sweets in a few swoops.

I would occasionally come upon one or another Lad in my travels.

And later on, too, although far less frequently. I did once chance on Crustacean sweeping out a greengrocer's shop several years later up in Camden Town. I recognized him more by his voice and mispronunciation of certain words than by his very clean and neat clerking apparel and demeanour.

"A parse-snip, yer see, is a moost delicate cretoor," he said, stroking it phallically at a comely kitchen maid. "Let me shoow you how to han'le it."

Another Grimmins Lad, Dungeness, some years later invited me to a steak pie and ale in a low Southwark tavern on Mint Street when I was extremely down in cash a time later. He and Little Tarpon—now named Big Tarpon—had joined a gang of young men, the Hell Boys of St. Mary Overy's Dock.

And it was another Grimmins Lad who would find me my occupation even later on, inside Tiger Jukes's house.

❖

I had become a child vagabond. Were I some German author, I would refer to these months after my dealings as a Grimmins Lad as my *Wanderjahre*, although I wandered less than a full year, running out of money despite husbanding it quite carefully.

Sunsets fascinated me, and I began to follow them. I wandered more westerly with each day to catch more of the sun setting. It had been summer when I decamped from the Dustbins for good. I contrived my way through a charming autumn and a despicable winter, and still I wandered.

The constabular phenomenon known as "bobbies," our version of urban gendarmes, had just begun then in force, and although they were not as popular as they have since become, they were sufficient and seemed to have little purpose but to move on young stalwarts such as myself with no visible means of support. Finding places to sleep in became more difficult, thus my wandering toward the bright newly built or rebuilt city areas like Westminster and St. Martins in the Square.

I had easily survived winter and early spring when I was of a sudden felled by an ague in mid-Spring of my tenth year. I remember roaming indecisively, wrapping my rags about myself continually: now too hot, now too cold, and at last finding myself lost in a great colonnaded plaza not far from the Strand. Here were ample doorways to *accoucher* myself, but many others filled them. I was too ill to find a berth using any force, so I crawled beneath some upended wooden crates, where I collapsed utterly. There I shivered myself into a febrile sleep, despite a makeshift blanket of grizzled ramps and torn chard leaves.

I awoke to find myself in Paradise. Or so it at first seemed. I must have slept most of the day unmolested beneath my cartons, for when I opened my eyes, they were sealed by sleep phlegm. Once opened, all was a blur, but I could still smell. And what I smelled were all the perfumes of the Indies, all the attars of the Promised Land, all the sachets of Heaven.

Angels were speaking, albeit in Cockney accents. After a while I could decipher one called Thalia saying I was damp feverish. Another named Zoe averred with some authority that I was about to perish. Both assured some elderly Seraph that I must be warmed and fed broth instantly. Thus I was lifted from my iced stone mattress of cobblestones and put into some kind of blanket-filled *crèche*.

Once there, I found myself so warm that I was soon deeply asleep again. I awakened after nightfall and made out many flickering fires within tin firepots circling my crib, which I now discerned was a rucksack-blanketed wooden slat crate in which large swedes are commonly packed for sale. Still, the lovely young girls before me were angels, and they fed me warm broth and carolled to me until I slept again, surrounded by the loveliest aromas in the world.

When I awakened fully, very early next morning, the aromas were still there, the angels barely visible, wrapped and sleeping in their makeshift beds. Their Aged Uriel was, in fact, a fellow named Theogones Herbert Newholl, "Florist Extraordinaire," according to the sign on his horse-drawn floral cart, which lay, hitches down, nag missing, upon the stones of the great square. He was no more than five-and-thirty years of age. I withdrew from my bed and unsteadily stood, seeing and hearing more approaching horse-drawn caravans like his, and

• 145 •

realized I had stumbled not into the Afterlife, but rather into the Covent Garden, the fresh produce and especially fresh-cut flower market of London supreme. Lilies, roses, daisies, mums, anemones, dahlias, straw flowers, and portias surrounded me, cut and moist in their shaved wrappings or water tins. Next to them pansies, francescas, peonies, and violets glowed within their clover-lined baskets.

Theo-Herbert sighted me first. "His Grace commences his levee," he announced portentously.

"I could eat your foot," said I, for it was days since I'd last eaten solid food, and his appendage looked particularly toothsome in its wrapped coloured stocking.

"Porridge might be had instead," said he. "Tepid or hot. Only a ha'penny for four bowls full. Just there, hark, where the steam and sweet wheat musk rises. But alas, I see Your Grace lacks a wallet. Doubtless you left it with your valet in a moment of forgetfulness." The two girls in the dray had awakened to our soft converse and giggled at his last words. "Might I have the honour, sir, of treating you this morn? Certain as I am that your repayment will be double, nay, treble, soon enough."

He was good enough to seat me in his wickerwork chair and to have a small lad fetch the gruel, which tasted like the most wonderful chop in the world. By then Thalia and Zoe were out of their bed in the little caravan where all three slept and were also hungry. No sooner had I fed myself than I was sleeping again, and so was lifted into one of their still warm, recently vacated sleeping places, where I passed most of that day.

Indeed, it was only the following morning that I was fully awake and able to assess my three saviours and their neighbourhood. What most amazed me was how soundly I had slept, for the din was colossal by day and only slightly less loud by evening. Unquestionably the several hundred people who gathered within the open-to-the-air elegant stone confines of "the Garden," as its familiars and I came to call it, at any single moment, accounted for it: speaking, shouting, laughing, brawling, seducing, cajoling, denying, affirming, despairing, elating, bargaining, refusing, imagining, and failing to imagine.

But 'twas the music that accounted for so much of it. I mean not the caterwauling in *solfeggio* practice of the tenors and soubrettes from the top open windows of the opera house ateliers that crowned the northeast external corner of the square, though those ariettas certainly added to the clamour. I mean the music of the flower and fruit sellers, the song of advertisement, the incantation of sale. Every seller had his or her own tune, volume, aphorism they each one sang out, all of their airs soon to be familiar to me.

My own newly adopted family—for the girls would not let Theo-Herbert toss me out—fit me in with their specifically Hellenic interests and even nomenclature. I was first nicknamed Somnus, after that Deity of Sleep, for what Theo-Herbert termed my "astonishing feats and adventures in the continent of slumber." But later, on when my arithmetical skills were noticed, I earned the far better name of Archimedes, or Archy, for short.

At first, as Somnus, I was put to work as soon as I could do so without feeling faint. Alongside the others I helped unlade from giant drays and sometimes even railroad cars stopped several streets away, the many, many trays of flowers, still deep in earth, sent to the market, purveyed thence directly from specific farmers and flower growers surrounding the city of London. These required one adult or two children to lift, but soon enough I showed off my strength by picking up and transporting at least the lighter ones all by myself. In this way, Newholl would get into the Garden faster than many of his colleagues. He was able to set up his stall first or second in his area, and thus attract sales from early customers out before breakfast to hopefully buy up large volumes of blooms for their picky mistresses in Marylebone or for their prickly, aging maters in Mayfair.

Some days there was more than one delivery made to the Newholls' dray site, and here I came in most handy, as I was able to assist Theo while his daughters stayed at our stall. As a rule, however, the girls were sent out to drum up sales on the very edges of the Garden, or into the northern and eastern thoroughfares outside it. Never too far, since Theogones was most fond of his offspring, and overanxious they remain safely unmolested, meaning he must be able to see them every few minutes, if only from a distance.

What had happened to their mother, his wife—referred to as Andromeda at odd moments—I couldn't at first quite penetrate through the facetious barrage of his Hellenified conversation, which spewed, leapt, gambolled, frolicked, and sparkled from his jolly, mutton-chop-fringed face. She must have been lovely as her namesake, since the girls were undoubted lookers.

Thalia, the older, was raven haired with porcelain skin and a grown-up woman's voice. Zoe, her junior by but one year, was rather more auburn and her complexion was more olive than not. Both girls bore their father's intelligent eyes and, though decorous, would, in a moment, break out into jokes and laughter, sounding for all the world like ale-wives. For this, too, I came to admire them.

And I admired them equally. Almost equally did I delight in their father. He never ceased to expatiate upon his instantly decided upon fiction that I was a fallen godlet or young baronet in disguise who had chosen, for his own amusing reasons best never too far delved into, to remain amongst them and the other hoi polloi, despite the obvious inconveniences entailed.

Theo-Herbert dealt with me as though with the most rational creature on earth. It amazed me and won me over. Of my general dirtiness when found, he assured me that "such a masquerade is no longer necessary." When I tried to wash myself in a horse trough, he laughingly plucked me by my filthy scruff and walked me to a public bathhouse, an invention of the Greeks, of course, he made it known, wherein he dropped me and had me soaped until clean. My rags, "a clever camouflage, though over-utilised, I fear," said Theo-Herbert, were burned. Cleaner, albeit possibly equally old, clothing from his own inventory of wear replaced it all. In some cases, barter at "the Garden" took place, swap after swap, until trousers of appropriately small waist were recovered. "Your Grace ought dine more often," Theo suggested mildly, adding, "This affectation toward extreme slenderness is no longer the fashion at Court."

I ate all that I could and all that I might, thanks to the money I was soon earning at the Newholls' flower stall. And how I spent it all was proof enough for Theo-Herbert that I was a born nabob since "only an heir apparent would not save a ha'pence, but eat sweets so regularly." Although the clincher for him in my fictional standing was when I could no longer hide the fact that I was able to read and write. "Here's a fine one," he assured his daughters. "Keeping his light under a bushel of parsnips."

Soon I was left in charge of the stall while the girls went out to the streets with cones of violets and packets of pansies, and Theo Herbert took his "afternoon siesta" in the 'van.

For close on two years I lived and worked in Covent Garden and soon had become part of their little family. Come holidays, we would hitch up to some elderly jade kept stabled not too many streets away, and we would make haste to entertain ourselves in some out-of-the-city inn in bad weather or some idyllic outdoors spot in a more clement climate. Theo-Herbert adored his daughters, who were good enough girls, I admit, but who for him walked on air like veritable fairies. Conversely, he scorned "young men," checking my face often to see if I had yet joined that hellish crew. Fair-skinned (I have black hair) though I am, I was still fairer then, and for a long time no hint of that ever-oncoming masculine tragedy was noted, despite his close inspection.

Slowly, and through the tattle of his fellow flower and produce vendors, I learned Andromeda Newholl was dead. She had been accosted by one of those blasted "young men" one afternoon when the girls were infants and Theo distant at work at the Garden. The scamp had fancied Andromeda and followed her home, and there he'd attacked her, had his way with her, and beat her badly when she resisted. She had lingered nigh on a week; in dying, she had broken her husband's heart. No other woman would ever do. Yet the girls grew, and somehow they became sufficient company. But while "boys and tots and lads" might easily gambol underfoot the Familia Newholl, "young men" like the criminal who had done in his wife and never been caught were not at all welcome. So, unless I might reverse Time itself, my days in this Floral Arcadia were numbered.

Those days came to a conclusion somewhat earlier than I anticipated, due to an incident regarding an elderly gentleman named Mr. Sloat. Sloat was an incompletely retired clerk, part-time supervisor over another dozen clerks in some nearby establishment. He was a tall, fatuous fellow, pear shaped, with a handsome if awfully narrow head above his usually bleached to blinding white neck cloth and a general decrease in cleanliness from the top down: a spotted lower coat, questionable trousers, with tattered gaiters barely still wrapped about his completely discreditable footwear. Sloat arrived three times a week between three and five of an afternoon. He invariably bought the same bouquet composed of gilly flowers, white stock, and to balance their economical cost, one gorgeous blossom, whether an especially large or fragrant red rose, a multi-blossomed tiger lily, or Harlequin tulip of superb size and colouring. His taste was by then so well established that Theo-Herbert, unpacking our flowers early each morn, would comment, "Now here's a centre bloom for Sloat."

As invariably as he arrived, so did Mr. Sloat short-change the girls should Theo-Herbert not be at the stall or if he were loudly asleep. He did this in a most annoying manner, giving Thalia, say, a sovereign for a large armful of flowers costing three shillings, and when she had given him the correct change, pointing out that she was a thruppence short. Embarrassed, she would add in the dull gleaming copper coin and curtsy, and Sloat would go off whistling, no doubt content with the universe now that he had cheated a hapless child out of three pennies.

Not only had he taken advantage of his age, size, and his position, he had done so very arrogantly, chiding the girl for her stupidity and barely accepting her heartfelt apologies. I burned witnessing it.

But there came an afternoon—Sloat always arrived after luncheon—when neither Theogones nor his daughters were at the stall but only myself. Sloat had seen me around enough of the time to not be put out by me at once. Again he gathered his bouquet, this time with a large pale blue iris as centrepiece. He handed me a sovereign, only to be met with my quick response. "Sorry, guv. No change of coin today. Mister Herbert 'as took it with 'im."

"Took it with him?" Sloat asked, as though I told him he'd turned water into wine.

"So he has," I said, holding a grip on the floral bunch he

wanted. "Mrs. Simon would give ye change, I don't doubt." I nodded in the direction of the woman at the next stall.

"Mrs. Simon?" asked Sloat, with such astonishment that I might have recommended Mrs. Beelzebub to him.

"'Fraid I mustn't leave the stall. Orders. Sorry, guv."

Well, you could have knocked Mr. Sloat over upon his very wide, soiled, *derrière*. Nevertheless, he went to her and obtained the change. We counted out the proper sum together, I quite loudly.

"Isn't it thruppence over?" he said.

"Why not take it back," said I, reasonably enough, handing it all back to him, "and we shall count it out again to be certain?"

He did so and of course he counted out and gave me the correct amount. With a very poor grace, I must say. Instead of his usual satisfaction, he walked away with a very grim down-turned mouth.

When Mr. Sloat did not appear the following day to take the large scarlet carnation Theogones had set aside for him, Theo-Herbert wondered aloud where he was. None of us had seen him. When Sloat didn't come a second day, I, of course, began to wonder. He did come a third day, but when he saw I was alone at the stall, he promptly turned around and took himself off.

Theo was just then awakening from his post-prandial nap and leapt after him. He cajoled Sloat back to the stall, waited on him personally, and sold him a gorgeous "black" tulip—actually night-time purple. Some time later that afternoon, he wondered at Sloat not appearing and then going away, and looked at me questioningly. I felt obliged to explain to him what I had done to keep Sloat from cheating me and why I had done so. I naïvely assumed Newholl would commend me upon my cleverness. Instead, he berated me quite loudly enough so a half dozen nearby flower and produce stalls could not have but heard his words.

Embarrassed and angry, I then in equally loud tones asked why it was that Theogones put up with Sloat humiliating his daughters so often.

"For the sake of his trade," said he. "Which is five days per week. In this way do I counteract his short-changing the girls."

But only by having the girls be told they were dolts.

"Girls *is* dolts," said Theo. "They can't count nor read and write like you nor I. What care you anyway how my daughters are humbled?"

I had no answer for that but to tell him I would no longer be party to such disgraceful behaviour, constant customer or not.

"Then find yerself another stall to sell at. And another crib to sleep in," he said, in equally affronted tones. "If yer so high and mighty."

For the next month or so, I did exactly that, filling in for other stalls' lads, or for their owners at the stalls during their lunch times or nap times. After such a long time there, I was, after all, familiar to all inside the Garden, and my reputation was fair enough. I had enough credit that I might have even opened my own stall, as Mrs. Simon urged me, looking to expand.

She also explained to me the real problem. "The gulls is growin' to become womens," said she. "And ye yerself, growin' to become a young man. He canna abide such."

So, while I worked enough to feed myself, more often I moped about the Garden from stall to wall, languishing upon kerb stone to slatted crate, fitted out with a slim volume of verse in my hand, fantastical as a Keats, languid as a Shelley.

Feigning the greatest ennui, in truth, I soon found

distraction enough. For a theatrical troupe suddenly arrived unannounced in Covent Garden late one breezy afternoon when all of us were going starkers chasing after our bonnets, hats, cash boxes, and stray stalks of airborne gladiolus.

The actors clangorously trundled into the square within two large, overblown, colourful, horse-drawn caravans, and immediately camped at the far north-eastern corner, where infrequent "entertainment" customarily set up stage.

The latter had, during my time there so far, constituted a wagon full of cheerless, fly-blown marionettes in so-called dramatizations of old legends that even Zoe Newholl disdained as puerile. I also recall an ancient *Punch and Judy* show, from somewhere in Essex, last costumed and painted up in the time of King George Second. Most recently, we'd been treated to a family dance company from Scotland purporting to be "Hebrides-bred and authentikal," of which the less said about it, the better for any future intercourse with our northern neighbour.

Monsieur Guillaume Darrot and The Invincible Theatre, read the man-sized placards of the new troupe, standing on either side of the little stage that was quickly erected between ends of two high-sided caravans parked six yards apart in the corner. Handbills distributed by myself, as a hired lad, named the individuals of the company, which besides M. Darrot included Mademoiselle Suzette Darrot, Mademoiselle Antoinette Genre, M. De Sang-Pur—doubtless the large, bearded, bald-headed fellow I had noted moving large objects about so much—and a "Grande-Madame de St. Clement-En-Hors-de-Combat," whom we were assured would play roles deemed "Domestic, Deistic, and Outlandish."

I laughed as hard as the other flower vendors, fruiterers and marrow-sellers, reading aloud for them this piece of Frenchified gallimaufry. Even so, two nights later, I joined an audience of several score, requiting my ha'pence for the troupe's first performance: *The Most Despicable and Horrible Tragedy of the Tyrone Family of —— County, Ireland*—after a tale written by that estimable Mr. *Joseph Bodin de Sheridan De Le Fanu*. And, like the other three score in the audience, I was terrified, frightened, and moved. Moved so much, in fact, that four days later and after having seen every one of their performances, I resigned the Covent Garden, flower-selling, and the Hellenically inclined Newholl family forever, and I joined The Invincible Theatre troupe.

There I would receive what might have been the first great polish to my education.

❖

M. Darrot turned out to be an individual no more exotic than a Mr. William Darrow, or Billy-Boy Dee, as his sire, another member of the troupe, one Jonathan Darrow, Mr. Pure Blood, or De Sang-Pur, called him. For all his age and his considerable airs, Darrow the Elder was no more well-born than your humble servant and hailed from some inconsequential townlet in Surrey.

And the purity of his blood, if it ever existed, must do daily battle with prodigious amounts of gin and usquebaugh to discover which liquid would prevail.

Still, the old reprobate was docile and had been for many long moons an actor with other troupes, including what remained of The King's Men during the realm of the last Regent, and so he had memorized his acting parts, or at any rate had gotten several resonantly long speeches by heart.

It was those speeches that Darrow the Younger had pilfered, and around them that he had since begun to scribble his own plays, far more popular adaptations of our then-contemporary literature as found in various three-volume novels and periodicals, along with those foreign dramas he happened upon and then lifted wholesale. Add to those two or three expurgations of Mr. Shakespeare filled with blood, thunder, ghosts, and revenge, and there you have the troupe's entire repertoire.

You may then easily guess that the great female dramaturge of the company, Mademoiselle Suzanne Darrot, was, in fact, Susie Darrow née Semple, wife to Billy-Boy. And Mademoiselle Antoinette Genre was, in truth, her niece by blood, a Miss Amy Green. As for the fifth member of the company, it would be many months before I uncovered that remarkable personage's complete identity and rather odd verity.

Meanwhile during their short engagement at the Covent Garden's out of doors corner, I had progressed with The Invincibles from being a mere set-up helper, to a placard boy, and on to becoming a constant "stage-handy lad," assisting Billy in setting up the changes of scenery. These commonly consisted of two parts: a painted background or, as they called it, "rear scrim," and a variety of deal or other lightweight wood furniture upon which the actors would perch and lean for verisimilitude, though few might actually hold the full weight of the somewhat rotund Darrow Elder for longish periods of time. I also drew the curtains to open and close the show as well as to register the so-called Entr'actes.

An immediate fascination with their art attracted me into the circle of The Invincible Theatre. Growing knowledge and increasing appreciation of their craft and all it comprised, indeed required, drew me even more tightly into their tiny realm. Thence, a kind of juvenile passion with those two lovely, and that one mysterious, female enmeshed me ever more.

Remember that I was at this time in that mid-age between boy and man that my former employer, Theogones, so abhorred. But I must admit that finally it was my total fixation upon Billy Darrow that at last folded me into the troupe's most intimate circle, for while I had before idolised members of the female sex, for the first time in my life, I found a male worthy of my uttermost infatuation.

Was he handsome, then, this leading actor, you will ask? Of course he was. He was a leading man of an acting troupe, after all. But then again, feature by feature, he was not especially remarkable. He had learned through stage makeup to over-benefit the advantages of his better facial features. His fine, glittering black eyes he emphasized by application of dark paint to his eyebrows and by thickening to ebony his eyelashes. His nose I knew for a fact at close sight to be slightly bent to the left. No matter, he painted a straight line down to its tip despite the bone and shaded it from either side, and it appeared ferrule-straight.

He re-limned and then daubed into the new outline his upper lip so it might be as voluptuous as its mate. He oh so softly rouged his cheekbones so they shone not quite so high, to make himself more cherubic for younger roles. Even so, later on, when a play-described "brilliant beau" was required for a walk-on role, Billy was the first to toss my own self, clad in gilt velvet with silver frogging, onto that never-very-steady movable stage in lieu of himself for the audience to ooh and aah over. True, his figure was slim and long, but almost, he believed, simian, with his somewhat apelike long arms and large hands. His posture was never quite Royal, unless it must be for a role. No, he was ever an indifferent King, preferring that his Elder or even the mysterious and multi-named fifth member take over those majestic roles when they were of a short duration.

As compensation, Billy was, however, most lithe, most flexible, and most assuredly athletic. He could juggle, he could somersault, he could leap high enough to make audiences gasp, and he would then just barely alight, one shaky foot atop a single shivering beam, his entire body vibrating as though he would topple over, and yet hold his ground steady, to everyone's amazed relief.

In short, he could, with no trouble at all, incur every viewer's eye by a score of differing means and hold it just as long as he wished. If his voice was nothing especial, a fair tenor, he could sing several airs of Mr. Handel and Herr Mozart with perfect tone and pitch, and he would leave a tear in your eye and a throb in your breast. But for the grand dramatic speeches, he must drag in that old sot, his sire, whose resounding baritone was a natal gift. So, as the lad Billy-Boy had watched his pater to learn, so watched I him every moment onstage, whether in rehearsal or "on show," to educate myself into what turned out to be an only middling grasp of the actor's craft.

And if Billy Darrow was admirable, he was even more so when he had someone to admire him. By this tenth year of The Invincible Theatre's existence, that meant no one other than myself. His wife was by then quite inured; his father was, as always, uninterested; and who knew what the fifth member thought, as we only heard uttered speech onstage. Even Billy's niece by marriage, his last conquest before me, was looking about for someone else to engage her esteem.

It was she, Miss Amy, who, three months into my employment with the troupe, made the discovery that despite all my larking about London town, among some of its most unsavoury haunts and disreputable gutters, that for sensual experience, at nearly twelve years of age, I was still "pure as the driven snow."

We had left London some weeks past and only just set up stage in the large, second common green of Sheffield town, and I had just returned from depositing our placards about those shop fronts that would countenance our adverts in their windows, when she faced me down. Her arms were akimbo, her chestnut hair all flying about, her cheeks reddened from proximity to the boiling hot water. In short, she looked quite notably natural for once and, if I must say so, quite lovely, too. The scene was the outdoor fire where she and her aunt were laundering the troupe's clothing in preparation for the week to come. By this time, I had come into a second set of shirt and trowsers, and so had given in my originals for cleansing.

"What's this, then?" she asked pointing to a stain no more remarkable to my eye than any other, except perhaps its location, slightly above the Y of my trowser legs. As I looked, she looked me in the eye and said, "Jizz, is what. Look, Ess, how he does stain himself at night."

I was unaware of staining myself at night or any other time and said so, unaware they were japing with me, until Mrs. Darrow asked, "Have you then no dreams at all, a lad your age, of ladies fair?" Upon which I blushed to recall one such dream about herself.

She laughed, but quickly enough the two of them calculated, and then said, "Haven't you ever…with a lass or lady?" And what was I to say? I turned and fled, murmuring some work that must be attended to immediately.

That night, my idol roused himself from his conjugal bed within caravan number one and came to where I had cobbled together my own more makeshift sleeping quarters on the street beneath caravan number two.

"Come, my love," he said, for that was how Billy spoke to all of us, my love, my darling, my sweetheart. "Come up to bed with Susie and me."

I was, to say the truth, amazed, for the cobblestones were especially iron-hard with ice that night with autumn coming on, despite my many efforts to disguise them with slats and cloths. Any softer lie-down would be preferable.

No sooner had we crept into the caravan and I was at the edge of the bed, viewing by faint candlelight Mrs. Darrow herself, all pink skinned, wrapped in warm covers atop softer pillows, than from behind, I felt his hands upon me. Before I knew what he was about, he'd stripped off my trowsers and shirt and pushed me atop her. From there, she took over, and any questions I may have uttered were stilled by first her and then him. Soon were we all three as Nature made us, and almost as quickly was I between her large soft breasts, being fondled and kissed, manipulated and managed from in front and in back by one and the other simultaneously, until I had found a wet harbour below and pushed to it. I found a rhythm and soon began to gasp. What heaven! Twice more did I consort with the distaff, while the husband consorted with the lady from behind, and alternately encouraged me with many caresses and lewd remonstrations. Through it all, I encountered and experienced so many differing sensations and emotions, that when it was all over, and the three of us were at last spent to our utmost, I lay between them both, and murmured my double adoration, before I collapsed into utter debilitation.

Once having tasted such delights, how then was I to be denied? I was not. From then on, for months on end, I bedded with my master and my mistress. True it was that the lady tired of our frolicks earlier some nights than the fellow did, and she would fall asleep, leaving Darrow to divert me. Increasingly as I appeared, I would in vain seek her, and be told she was sharing Amy's bed that night. Or more simply, "Getting her much-needed sleep, for she worked hard today, two shows and three parts, and she knows she'll get little enough sleep with you about." This was said sternly, just before he kissed my lips and rifled my undergarments with his monkey-quick hands.

In vain did I attempt to draw Miss Amy into our nocturnal diversions. "Leave her be, the poor thing," Susie would say. "Haven't she enough of menfolk during the day?" This latter was not so much directed at myself, who outside of the bed at caravan one remained as shy and diffident as before. Nor did it refer to our leader, much as I would come upon him all unawares staring at the lass when she knew not he was about, and he surely appeared to have more than theatrical ambitions upon his mind.

No, but it did allude to Mlle. Genre's slow but certain new appearance, her growth, both physical and dramatic, lending her far greater stature and her experience, providing greater repute, so that when his wife complained of too much labour, our Billy Boy simply transferred the roles to his niece. Amy took them on with a loud enough grumble and a demand for "more meat and less gristle," but despite these noises, in truth she played the new parts joyfully and acquitted herself very well indeed. So well, in fact, that she acquired admirers by the by. Indeed, by the time we had arrived as far as Nottingham Shire, Mlle. Genre could rely upon several gentlemen's carriages to be parked just outside the circle that comprised our audience, the owners seated upon fold-out seat contraptions prepared by their valets or drivers, near enough to the stage where they might admire Amy from closer quarters—an advantage for which Darrow charged a half shilling per head. I would not have been amazed to have closed down in one town and set up for travel to another and seen our little tripartite retinue followed by another entire and quite longer cortege of Amy's guest-admirers.

"They used to follow *me* so," Susie whimpered very early one morning, when we three had shared a bed together again.

The back curtains of the 'van formed a little V out of which I could see the pre-dawn constellation Cassiopeia clearly against the cobalt night.

Her husband soothed her, holding her tight about as she sobbed on. "Even more admirers than she. Even higher born. Do you remember, Billy?" He did remember, loyal mate that he was, and he said so. They reminisced about Lord This and Baron That until she was mollified a bit, at which she caught sight of me and declared, "Does it never go down? I ask you, truly. Never? Ah, well, at least *one* handsome lad admires me." She turned to cover me with her soft form, so I was forced to somewhat awaken, while Darrow added his own domestic admiration from behind her.

I mentioned triple 'vans because we had gained a third, somewhat smaller and older than the others and thus in a more parlous state, yet withal useful, because that's where Darrow the Elder, and the silent and apart from us but for the stage Fifth Troupe Member now slept and kept their costumes and other belongings, Susie having moved many of hers to be with Amy. So I now had a home up off the cobblestones, and while it was not my own bed, it was the first of such an object since I was an infant.

Partly this was ascribable to our increased "box office," as the nightly monetary receipts were euphemistically spoken of, there being a box, if no office. Amy's increase of new followers were partly responsible for that boon, but so, it turned out, was I. For I soon became a performer in The Invincible Troupe myself, and if I may be immodest, a not terribly unimportant addition to the company, especially to the lasses and womenfolk, for I too had grown, almost as tall as Darrow, and had sprung soft down upon my lip and cheek and chin, which Susie and even Billy did fawn upon.

The manner of it coming to pass was thus: I have written

of how I had slowly accustomed myself to the boards—and boards indeed they were, eight of them of the same thickness and width, that I myself put up and took down along with Billy Darrow. I had gone onstage first in the various non-speaking roles that Darrow's repertoire called forth.

In one act was I a silent Royal personage before whom a duel would be fought, or in another a judge, with but one word to utter—"guilty" or "released." For these I naturally enough took upon myself the colouring that stage powders and paints could provide, and I appeared stern or elderly or authoritative as the role called for. No sooner was my one word said or my four gestures made than I was off the stage and returned to my duties as stage-handy lad moving about this or that scrim or prop—short for furnished property, or the objects needed for the play. On occasion, as I've also written, I was a great beau or fop, costumed with extraordinary style and panache but with little to say or do.

Even in the most stalwart of troupes, actors "go down"— get ill, or depressed, or vanish two days on end with some townsperson, or refuse to leave their caravan from "a case of the sulks." Our fifth ordinarily silent troupe member was the first to become ill, with a catarrh that interfered mightily with her ability to speak *sans* a cough. She did lovely work of hiding it or stitching it into the scenes she played, just as though it belonged there. At least she did the first two nights. The third night proved impossible for her to get out of bed or leave caravan three for her feverish state, and thus was I cast in her place.

The play was the Bard's *Tragedy of Romeo and Juliet*, and the most unlikely part I was to take over for her was the small role of Lady Montague, Romeo's mother, with but a handful of lines. The largest role I must slip into in her stead was that of Mercutio, playing to Billy as my best friend. I had learned by heart the two speeches already: one fantastical and the other pathetic. Later on, I was to play gruff Friar Laurence, and what lines I was unsure of would be whispered to me by someone or other in the company offstage at the time.

In the first role of the young smart, I japed much with Darrow, who played Romeo and who, in turn, flirted back at me, giving a new significance to these young men's close friendship in the play. This impelled one Oxonian within the audience to laugh out loud, "Why! Look! They are as *Greek* as ever were *Italian lads*! And I'll wager as prompt at each other with their *cods* as with their *daggers*!" a comment that earned much merriment. Later on, as the Friar, my beard did itch badly, as did my monk's cowl, and I was eager to be rid of those, but the applause was delightful, and when Mercutio was called for, I vanished and reappeared *sans* beard and blanket but wearing the other's doublet and feathered hat, and bowed to even greater kudos.

Later that night, as we sat in the local public house gobbling down our late and by no means undercooked dinner, 'twas Susie who said of me, "He's bit. Why, look. As surely as though it were a gadfly upon his neck, he's bit by the streaming limed-lamps, he's fired up himself and by the yokels' hand claps—stage-bit, the great dolt!"

I coloured deeply, for it was not entirely untrue.

Darrow Elder, who seldom spoke once his tankard was in hand, deigned to utter to me, "A capital Queen Mab, lad." Then pondering. he added, "A somewhat less creditable death speech." Which drove us to hilarity, for he could not give aught, not even words, but he must take something back.

After that night, I remained onstage with The Invincible Theatre troupe, earning my own sobriquet, Monsieur Addison Aries, a name conjured by the Darrows, husband and wife, out of my given name and an old *Astrological Almanack* one of the company had snitched somewhere in Northern Wales and which they followed closely. They were a superstitious lot, all of them, our mysterious fifth (now sixth) actor included. None of the women stepped onstage without first spitting behind herself and twirling her index finger in a curlicue while uttering below her breath, "Pig's foot!"

Though none could tell from whence it all derived, the elder Darrow would not call a single playwright by exact name, but rather referred to one as "The Immortal Bard," and "The French Rapscallion" for Molière—whose Scapin we travestied rather absurdly. Novelists that we adapted likewise underwent a sea-change, from Dickens to "Frick'em," for example, and when once I had come upon and was reading a single volume novel about the Antipodes titled *Harry Heathcote of Glangoil*, the old thing took a look at the author's name and said, "Anthony Scollop, is it? I read once a book by him—concerning a Mrs. Prudie!" To which I smiled and made myself scarce, for Darrow Elder being friendly was more frightening by far than him being his usual drunken self.

And so, My Lord, I passed my thirteenth, fourteenth, and fifteenth birthdays as Mercutio and Tybalt, as Friar Laurence and Lady Montague, as Lord Marchmell and the Duke of Tickles, as Raggs the Sheep-herd and Stiggs the Scrivener, as Charles Surface, and Young Dornton, as Captain Absolute and Sir Derleth Tyrone the Younger, as Doctor I. M. A. Dandy and Mlle. Camille du Sprech, as Young Fool and Old Liar, as Unknown Bandit, and First Soldier, once even as Lord Beverley, and twice as Lord Mayor of London; but in short, as a repertoire-actor.

For Billy Darrow was no fool and knew that whatever extra I earned from him on the boards trebled in farthings, quickly gaining for that new Invincible Troupe actor, M. Aries, his own little "claque," or so one's followers are named. I was furthermore useful in so many other ways to his company: as stage worker, as tender lover to his wife, who thus minded less her usurpation in the company by her niece, and thus didn't make the expected trouble, and not least of all useful as Billy's own personal Antinous, for I was rich with spunk, and he was determined to mine it out of me one way or t'other.

❖

In retrospect, those were my golden years. Ah! If only I had appreciated them more at the time. But like most youths, I was drawn to the Mysterious. Unfortunately, one rather perplexing mystery faced me nearly every day. Solving that mystery would be utterly enlightening to me, but it would also, alas, prove my undoing.

I have mentioned before the *sixth* member of The Invincible Travelling Theatre. But I have always done so mysteriously and for good reason. Mysteriousness seemed to hover about this troupe member from morn 'til night, despite the greatest illumination thrown from a beneath a fire-lighted lime-light.

I have said this actor played both male and female. No surprise when so did I, as did Amy Green. I have also said this actor possessed a voice of surpassing range. Singing from a higher soprano than Suzie Darrow down to bass notes our senior-most fellow, old Jonathan Darrow, might encompass. Recall that they boarded together in one wagon, yet utterly apart; and it did not signify that anyone knew the better nor associated the more with this Theatrickal Enigma.

More than once did I ask Billy Darrow who this *Personne de Grand-Chance* might be, in truth.

"Leave it be, Addison, my love, for no good can come of your needing to know."

"But surely that person is not of the Darrow kith and kin."

"That is so."

"Then how came this person to your troupe?"

"By slow degrees. By a downfall from a greater estate," Billy said. We were pulling up stakes for the tented enclosure against poor weather that some folks paid a shilling extra for. "But surely, a smart lad like yourself has already discovered that."

"You mean because of this person's great adaptability?"

"That, too. But who else among us can hold an audience so completely rapt?"

"Why, yourself," answered I, ever loyal. "With your tumbles and leaps and tricks."

"Aye, that foolishness—and only betimes."

"And your sire, too, with his tragic speeches."

"All five of them, when he chooses to be sober."

"And Miss Green, when she wears her bodice low upon her bust and flirts."

"And yourself for all that, when you are dressed in gold and well peruked and flirt with the ladies in the second row," he said. "But surely you've noted how different our Great Person to be?"

I had and yet could not put it into speech, so I held my own.

"Do not be bothersome to anyone in the troupe, Addison, or I shall have to whip you, too, among the many fleshly duties I already manage."

So was I warned.

By this time we had begun a new play, Mr. Shakespeare's *Twelfth Night*, much expurgated, given our audiences and their general understanding, chopped back to no more than two hours, albeit full of wit and flirtation.

Nowhere more so than between the maid, Viola, dressed

as a man to court the noble Olivia for Duke Orsino, and Olivia herself. Who then mistakes Viola's stranded brother, Sebastian, for her as Cesario and forces him to wed her.

We had rehearsed this, myself as Sebastian for The Invincibles, but most of all playing opposite Suzie, with whom I had been second husband for nigh two years by now, and with whom I felt most congenial.

All the more of a surprise then, when "Mlle. Genre" came down with a rotten tooth and could not play the opening. And an even greater surprise that Suzie Darrow would then play Viola, a role she knew well, and our fifth person then "took over" the role of Lady Olivia, evidently having been several roles in the play in previous years. Or decades. I knew not which.

This I discovered as I made the announcement of the parts and the cast, that is to say, before the curtain, and upon opening day, in a rather large market square at the town of Croydon.

I then ran backstage, where I was fitted into my first costume and went on in my first role as retinue to old Jonathan's Orsino. Billy played Toby Belch and Antonio and other clownish roles.

Our mysterious sixth actor as Olivia flirted believably and also gave the part emotion, and even evoked tears in the cheeks of the females of the audience with her sad plight. More than one of them had loved a youth and not been loved in return. Suzie as Viola/Cesario played charmingly and affectingly, too.

So we arrived at Act Four, Scene One, before Olivia's house, where I as Sebastian have arrived and now seek to rid myself of Billy's clown. He returned in a minute as Sir Toby, and we had at each other with soft-sticks, stopped by Lady Olivia's importuning words.

She has only just noticed Sebastian and thinks him

Cesario. Billy had cut that act's second scene and so here we are at Scene Three, and all of a sudden, Lady Olivia begins making love to Sebastian. He, being a healthy youth, responds to her beauty and advancements. Passionately and loving, we troth our pledge, and Sebastian is dragged off to a parson to be married. I well knew to play this part ardently and adoringly.

Astonish me, then, when our mysterious sixth drops all the reserve that had surrounded her with mystery. She grasps my hand tightly, clasps me about the body tighter, stage whispers insinuating and lovingly, and then kisses me so deeply I thought I might lose my wits. I looked baffled, as fitted Sebastian in the play, but in reality, too. One who had never before as much as regarded me now seemed to have adored me from afar, and only just then allowed me to understand that. Rustlings among the front seats showed that they too had intuited or somehow understood the real passion exerted betwixt us. From the backmost standees came low whistles and even a growl or two, marking me as a "lucky dog."

Nor was I physically released during the short scene behind the curtains, but held ever more closely, with much hand fumbling about my person, so that I stuck out like some fool jackanapes, until I put my clothes in order in time for the final scene in which Viola and Sebastian are re-united and the Duke and she become as one, while Sebastian and Olivia retroth our pledge and all exeunt, leaving Billy all alone to sing, "When I was a tiny little boy, with a hey-ho, the wind and the rain."

Behind the curtains once again, I turned to our mysterious sixth and said, "Tonight. A ten o'clock. Be certain old Darrow is dead drunk." She responded with a hand upon my manhood.

And so, as the clapping endured—and we two were especially applauded—was that stage that has been my life, and I do not mean that little makeshift stage that was The Invincibles Theatre—set for its next quite dramatic act and transformational scene.

❖

How inflamed I was after that provincial premiere of Billy's expurgated *Twelfth Night* you may easily imagine. Seldom have I been quite so heated.

The hours I had to wait dragged by like Eternity itself, and it was all I could do to not drink myself ale-blind, as we four, Suzie, Billy, Jonathan, and myself, celebrated our quite substantial take from our performance in a local pub, named—and this is one of those coincidences that makes my life so piquant—the Fallow Deer. Naturally, Billy was looking forward to future performances. We were already the talk of the town, especially as several townsfolk did stop by our table and ask for a repeat the following night. More cheer followed that, you may be assured.

At last we all wandered away to our wagons, Jonathan drunk, Billy and Suzie cordially tipsy, and myself in a quiet frenzy of anticipation, albeit acting as though I too was inebriated.

So, they pushed me into sick Amy's wagon, where she slept snoring away and none too clean smelling neither, while they celebrated with a rare husband and wife cohabitation.

As the 'vans were placed together in one side corner of a minor lane of the main square, I could, by peeping out of the curtains, sometimes even see what took place in the other two. Thus, at ten o'clock sharp by the local steeple bells, I was on the flagstones outside the smaller 'van, as washed and close to undress as I dared be, making my whistle-signal to the *Grande Personne* herself.

Naturally, the interior was dim-lit, a mere candle-end set upon a carton of costumes that served as a bed stand. Through the wooden partition, I could easily hear the stentorian gasps and wheezing, snores, and assorted harrumphs of old Jonathan in his sleep.

And there lay my Love, all soft and white-skinned amid her furled bedclothes. Her hair lay in shining ringlets upon her noble neck and tumbled a bit upon one ivory shoulder. I might easily make out the softly ridged concavity of her back, guarded as it was by her two pillowy softnesses. She turned an unpainted face toward me and with one finger, *soubrette* style, to her lips bade me be very quiet.

She lay like that while I removed my shirt and trowsers— I'd come barefoot—as though musing, and she seemed most pleased, as she reached for my extremity which greeted her so avidly.

Soon enough I was atop her and fondling. Unlike Suzie or even Amy, she was slender rather than voluptuous, smooth-skinned, but free of that padding wherein I might lose myself after passion. Her breasts were small and almost firm but were as much her weakness as any other female once I had them well in hand. Soon enough was I hand-guided to her lower regions and there she equalled Suzie well enough.

As onstage, her kisses were intoxicating, and I will even use the oft-repeated term breath-taking. At times, I believed I might never recover my breath unless I detached myself from her lips. I did so less and less as she guided me within herself, and from atop and behind her I began my manly ministrations.

Believe me, My Lord, when I report I never had encountered before and seldom since such passion from a partner in love-making. Most ladies merely *receive* a gentleman, some with greater motion than others, few with such enthusiasm and even athleticism and unstanched hunger.

Quickly enough, despite my efforts, did we rise and fall toward that bliss that is common to all. Much as I resisted, much as I had been taught by Suzie and Billy Darrow to resist, all teaching went for naught in that bed. Nor were either of us satisfied even then, but we must start up again for a second time, and while that lasted longer, and we rose to new feats of intertwining, never mind conclusion, did even that suffice, but we tried a third time.

If I seem somewhat muddled in the telling now, My Lord, you may well imagine how utterly fuddled with longing and lust was I at the time. And so I shall attempt to write it as I recall, precisely and in order.

Firstly, we had risen off the mattresses and now were standing up, my mistress holding on to the curved upper bars of the caravan for support, myself holding on to her chiefly, also grasping an overhead strut every once in a while.

As I was riding my way into my final *voyage de amour*, one hand cupping her breast slid downward. To it I joined my second hand and just as the great heat was upon me, it slipped further down and encountered—how can I write it?—manhood as large and stiff as my own. And inches below, a distinctive womanhood.

I gasped quite loudly. At the same time, I felt myself drawn in ever more deeply and closely. She spent. I spent. And all the while I had one hand on her manhood and another upon her womanhood.

In that same instant, the partition shook and splintered, and Jonathan Darrow himself, wide awake and bulging red with drink, thundered, "Must you? Must you? Must you yet *again*?"

His complaint was stopped by the vision that even a vat of ale and a decanter full of Scots whiskey could not undo: the vision, that is, of ourselves, standing before him *in flagrante* and possessing not two but instead three sets of genitals.

"What then…What demons be ye?" he added, doubtless quoting lines from some play we knew not. And he fell over the partition on to the bed alongside us.

My companion pulled free and leapt to the bit of floor where clothing was tossed all about until some semblance of costume was put on. I stood there in great astonishment, clad as I was the minute I was born. Jonathan rose in his fusty bedclothes and lurched toward me. I fought him down and rushed out of the 'van following my partner who, now dressed, had alighted and stood in a defending posture, looking like a very Achilles in those prints by Mr. Flaxman.

Roused by the great noise, Billy and Suzie and even Amy had looked out of their curtains, just as Jonathan tumbled out of the 'van and lunged toward me, only to be stopped by a perfectly aimed and quite powerful full-fisted blow to the nose by my lady transformed into man.

Soon, those in the pub's inn chambers nearby had thrust up their window sashes, and the scene was there for all to see.

My hermaphrodite pushed past me once more into the 'van, thrusting my clothing at me, where it fell upon the cobbles, and in a minute had run to the front exit and leapt on one of the old bays kept there un-shafted and roused it with a kick. Minutes later, we witnessed our sixth actor riding upon it, bareback as any American Indian or Amazon warrior, off across the square of Croydon into the frosty night.

By this time, the entire plaza and surrounding streets were lighted up, as I pulled on my trowsers. Folks were shouting and calling jibes at us, throwing down objects upon our heads.

"Damn your hot blood!" Billy Darrow rushed out at me. "Didn't I tell you *not to*?"

Luckily, he stumbled in his ill-timed charge at me.

In short time, I was up and inside, past Suzie and gathering my belongings and pay.

By the time I was upon the ground again, it was in time to hear Billy railing, "You've ruined everything. Everything! Everything!"

Still not fully clad, I pushed on my shoes as best as I could, and then I blew Suzie a kiss, and I too sped off, in the direction of the most surprising lover of my life…although toward where exactly, and what I expected to find, I could not say.

❖

From just outside of Croydon-town north to London is not far, and while fatigue soon approached my walking thither, so did an elderly farmer, who offered me a ride in a dray laden high with split-ricks of horse feed. I could not help but note that all the while, he looked carefully at my face and my theatrical costume. The former was still not free of the greasepaint of the night's performance, and the latter rather more elegantly turned out than is common among those he might be expected to regularly encounter at so small an hour upon the road.

I explained my predicament as well as I might, which gained his laughter and eventual help.

He left me near the King's Yard in Deptford, where his business of the morn lay, and he was good enough to arrange for me to travel onward farther than I might have dared hope, through Upper Kent, upon an acquaintance's dogcart, up to Halfway House. Once arrived, I dropped off, tipped the fellow a penny, and was left to my own devices.

Although I'd asked as often as we encountered others

coming against us on the roads or whenever we must stop, no one had seen my Amazon. So it was, with a growing, sad belief that I had lost forever those so ambivalent charms, that at sunrise I took to my tuppence bed at Halfway House, that noted inn.

I awakened late at noon and was immediately assailed by two strong odours. One, quite unpleasant, was due to the retraction of the Thames River tide, only several streets distant. The other was an equally strong and thus countervailing delicious aroma of Arabian coffee being brewed. From the height of the inn's placement, I might look across the flats of East Rotherhithe to the Thames's largest bend south, and across it to the India Docks and Isle of Dogs. So I found myself quite near to London itself, place of my birth and of my earliest years.

Even so, it was a very different scene from that I'd appreciated only hours before—I mean the deep green lawns and flowered country lanes about the town of Croydon—that I must have sighed rather more theatrically than my new companions were accustomed to hearing. Indeed, our view was of a grey and rainy day. Sleet crossed the face of the mullioned windows in slow gales. The vista they gave upon even the best of days was, however, oppressive: miles of double-storey dockside warehouses. The river presented its least prepossessing prospect here, and upon its other bank lay only more of the same dreary warehousing, interspersed with thrown-together hovels and other constructions of iron used, I supposed, for lading.

"Cheer up, lad," the slavvy in her food-stained apron said. "Since you had coin, you'll break fast well here at Halfway House. Fresh baked bread, Irish pertaters baked and topped in a buttered slab, three fat toasted rashers, a half slice of tomater…what do you say also to an egg?"

I said that it sounded to be a Lupercullan feast and soon sat down to it.

Imagine my astonishment, if you will, when several minutes later I had only just wiped the egg off my chin, who should saunter down the stairs and into the public room but a lanky fellow with hair as orange as one of those Spanish mandarins.

Though youthful, he had the casual yet elegant air that declared he was living off five hundred a year in railroad shares. He also possessed a voice, that once heard, I could never forget.

"Eeer now, me blandished female of pulchritude," says the newcomer in greeting to the semi-stupefied lass pouring him coffee. "I'll need as large a repast as possible this day."

In vain did she offer him her bill of fare: kippers, herring, potatoes and tomatoes. He waved them off as "Fer mere riff-raff." Eggs, bread, bacon, and ham also were dismissed out of hand. He had had "a regular laborious night of it," averred he, and what he wished—his grey-blue eyes all a glitter—was nothing less than a "beefsteak with all the trimmin's. And don't yer skimp on the gravee none."

After she had left for the larder, he smelt his coffee and sipped it as though he were the grandest Turk among the Ottomans. He had made short work of it when he deigned to notice myself quite openly staring at him. He then cocked one flame-coloured eyebrow over a suddenly inquisitive eye.

"Do I *know* you, sir?" he asked, loudly, and in the most provocative tone of voice possible, to the otherwise empty taproom.

"I believe you *do* know me, sir!" I responded, equally aggrieved.

Now his two burning bright eyebrows fought for which might reach his hairline first, he was so irate and perplexed.

"Have we had *words*, sir?" asked he, fuming.

"Upon a time, we did indeed have words. And slept together too. Arm in arm, legs pressed against each other," I added saucily.

He retained his surprisingly cool demeanour, especially after having been given such extreme provocation.

"Indeed, sir, you are extremely young to afford the services that are provided by Mr. Alistair MacIlhenny the Third."

Here he peered at me closely.

It was all I could do not to burst into laughter.

"Perhaps so, sir," I replied. "But at the time, your sleeping services went for less than nothing, as you were yourself so young." And as he blinked at me, I added, "And you were at that time hailed by the name of Lobster Tail."

He all but knocked over his coffee cup.

"Yer don't say so! Then art yer one of the Grimmins Lads? I thought yer face familiar, albeit too clean for any certain identification."

He stood up and approached my table. "Let me guess, Little Tomallalley, is it? Or rather Lil' Tarpon? Wait! I know who? That voice!" He pretended to ponder, listening to some invisible interlocutor. "Ne'er Cockney, always a bit larned." He turned to me in triumph. "'Tis Scallop. Why! Scallop! It is, 'tisn't it?"

Here we both rose and clasped hands and shoulders, and he joined me at my deal table, where he explained neither his alias, nor a great deal else, at least not immediately.

I drank more coffee while his meal, more apt for evening than morning, arrived and as he tucked into it, I was once more taken by how such a slender lad could put away such large quantities of food. He had done so as a boy, taking four meat pies, not two like the rest of us Grimmins Lads, and two fat brown loaves not one, and always making fast work of them.

We exchanged our histories—or at least in my case a somewhat expurgated version of the same. Here, across the river from London town, it had already become evident to me that should I ever perchance come across The Person whom I'd lost and still sought, it would be completely circumstantial. In a city of a half-million souls, s/he was as lost to me as a ha'penny at the Seven Dials crossroads.

"Then yer cannot return to the te-atter?" MacIlhenny said, more than asked, after I had explained my predicament.

"Not that theatre, at least. Certainly not. And who knows but in a few weeks' time the word will have gotten about of my misadventure. And I shall be barred from all such establishments."

"'Tis a shame," Lobster Tail declared with a frown. "I do like a good play, mesself, and I would've so enjoyed seeing yer tread the boards all costumed up as a pirate or maid. But as yer now unemployed and I suppose seeking some of the same, p'raps I may have a proposition to dangle afore yer?" said he.

"I am eager to hear," said I. "Are you self-employed?"

"Nay. But I am *well employed*." He looked about to see that no one was listening, then added conspiratorially, "By none other than Tiger Jukes!"

"Tiger Jukes?"

"Not so loud. Not so loud. The Tige prefers to be known but not well known, if you see what I mean."

I didn't but shook my head anyway. "In what capacity?"

"Rum."

"Rum to drink?"

"Aye, some of that, but all of what Tiger Jukes operates and manages is damnably rum!"

By which I gathered that Tiger Jukes was a master criminal of sorts and Lobster Tail now one of his gang of crime-fellows.

"In what capacity?" I repeated with real interest.

"Why, Tige's got the 'extras' of the docks sewed up tight, does Tige. From China Hall to Jamaica Row and all of the docks of the Driff in betwixt, not one single spot of cargo is pilfered but Tiger Jukes isn't behind it or doesn't receive a percentage of it."

"And this is how you eat beefsteaks for breakfast?"

"Well, never mind I, Scallop, me lad. Yer shall be eatin' them soon enough. I shall take yer to Tiger Jukes mesself."

There was the little matter of him paying his tariff, which Lobs—I mean MacIlhenny—settled by grandly saying, "The genl'mun upstairs shall pay it all. As usual."

Laughing at my befuddlement at this mystery, he grasped my arm and led me forth.

We strode on in the decreased drizzle, two great lads, well fed, and with pence in our pocket. Pounds carried I, wrapped tight beneath my more naturally acquired prized possessions. We walked toward where we could make out Wapping, across the turbid waters. The rain had abated only a little by then.

There, upon a neighbourhood not extremely different from that we had just left, if more ancient, seemingly erected during the time of Charles the Murdered King, we came upon those mansions, somewhat the worse for wear from the eternal southerly winds known as Folly's Ditch that blew off Jacob's Island.

Amid the twists and turns of the various lanes, one larger and somewhat more restored edifice rose upon Rope Lane and Rotherhithe Road. Before this better-looking establishment, three Bravos idled, coming to stand tall once we had approached across the lane. Recognizing my companion, they sat themselves down again and proceeded to idle once more, playing mumble-the-peg and swearing at the results.

"'El-lo, Mac," said the tallest, roughest, and least scarred of the three, an Irishman of so snub a nose once might roll coins upon it and they would gather but not fall, of hair so strong and straight and black that were it not for his high complexion and green eyes, one might take him for a Portaguee.

"'El-lo, Dunphy. Is the Tige up and about?" Lobs asked.

"Holding' 'er usual levee, Mac." Then looking me over, "Who's this, then?"

"A friend."

"A house-lad, you mean to say."

"I said a friend," MacIlhenny insisted.

Dunphy moved back, but as I passed in through the foyer said, "Ye'll be dining on Irish sausage yet," which I thought an excellent prophecy, as I was partial to sausages.

The restored grandeur of the exterior of this manse was duplicated within, and soon we arrived at a curved stairway dropping down into a *fleur-de-lis* papered hall. There sat a heavily painted and cheerful woman, her figure all but hidden in a gigantic flowery chintz *pelisse*, her high hair all but secreted within dozens of paper curlers. She sat at a fine, almost spindly, French-looking table upon which tea in bone china and half-eaten pasties were placed.

Several men were seated in chairs before her or standing and listening to her carefully, as her voice was low and rather sweet. My companion held me in the rear of the crowded room, only crooking a finger when she happened to look in our direction. I noticed a lovely pair of large, almost saucy, black eyes, and the once pert features of a *soubrette* as she looked myself over.

As they all spoke in a low tone of voice, all I might make out were various expressions of astonishment and dismay from the men, while she remained ever level and even-toned. At last their business was concluded, and the fellows all made for the exit.

She now crooked a finger at us, and Mac pushed me forward.

"Mrs. Athaliah Jukes," said she, swanning toward me a not unattractive hand. She made a moue, and I knelt to buss her chubby pink hand.

"Mr. Addison Grimmins," I said, causing Mac to let out and then suppress a laugh.

"Please sit, Mister Grimmins," she said, offering me but not Lobster Tail a seat. It was he whom she addressed, however. "Dear young Mister MacIlhenny, it does my heart much good to see that you have taken my advice into your ordinarily heedless head and have at long last brought to me someone who may do great good for us all, and who may make both my and his own fortune."

I thought this a good opening and was about to speak, when she placed a perfumed finger across my lips and continued on to him.

"We know that your own attributes, Mister MacIlhenny, are, while few in number, centred upon a prodigality of nature!"

She giggled, and Lobs coloured.

"But whatever young Mister Grimmins's own male attributes may be are of far less moment to us, since he is of a personal beauty, of a personal *classical* beauty that I have not seen in this house since that moment when I myself was fortunate enough to be carried across that threshold. Upon my wedding day, young sirs. By the late Mister Jukes. And shortly thereafter had that portrait taken."

She pointed to an upper wall of the hall. There I made out a portrait which might be construed as herself, quite young, half settled upon a settee of pink satin, with at her feet several black pugs in beige paw-shoes.

"He has come to join us in our quieter dock work," MacIlhenny now said in a tight voice.

She flounced up to her feet and, once risen, she proved to be unexpectedly large and most rotund.

"No. No. *NO. NO!* You're *quite* mistaken, Mister MacIlhenny. Quite! Does one *toss* a rare Brazilian orchid into the *gutters* of Rope *Lane*? Of course not. Mister Grimmins, may I call you Addison? Whatever Mister MacIlhenny so monstrously *intended* by introducing us, I assure you I have in mind a far greater destiny for you."

"Not a house-lad?" Lobster all but strangled out the words.

"May I remind you," she said grandly, yet firmly, "that *you* have been and still are a house-lad, and if I must say so, one of the most *popular* in the history of this house? Perhaps," she added darkly, "it is time that you should quit that occupation yourself—to your *youngers* and betters—and move on to other labours more like quiet dock work."

"I meant..." Mac had paled somewhat. "I'd prefer not."

"Naturally, you would prefer not," she said. "And so I supposed. Yet, tell me Mister MacIlhenny, how much were your earnings yester day and night?"

"Three shillings four pence."

He held it out, and she promptly took the coins and dropped them down into her décolletage.

"And yet, Mister MacIlhenny, I recall a date in the not so recent past when your prodigal gifts were wont to bring in six shillings per day. Regularly."

"I had a large meal," he added somewhat shamefacedly.

"However, neither *I* nor this house did share in that meal," she said, "And so it is immaterial."

She waved him off, and he retired to a corner of the large chamber, where I occasionally heard him throwing a knife into an old chest.

She, meanwhile, spent the next ten minutes doing her best to charm me.

I would remain in the house, she told me, and never—like my friend—need go out of doors upon "calls." Naturally enough, I would have all the time in the world to myself when not at the house and much freedom and two, no three full suits of new clothing, all bespoke down to my undergarments. I would dine like the Duke of Bedford and—

"Doing what ? For what would I be paid, ma'am?"

"Not very much work at all as far as the actual labour goes," she said, glibly enough. "And certainly not as much as if you were a quiet dock worker, which can, at times, after all, be extremely hard work, and at other times even perilous work as it is, you understand, a species of pilferage." She giggled and then darted another question at me: "You possess how many years, young Addison?"

"Eighteen."

"Come, come, Mr. Grimmins! Do these glowing orbs seem to you so utterly blind? Again I ask. Or better yet, shall we estimate—fifteen and a half years?"

I admitted it.

"Then you shall have seven, perhaps eight excellent earning years. And because of your gift, we shall split your take down the middle."

I heard Lobster Tail snort something from within his niche.

"Since," she now said loudly, "I shall easily be able to charge *double* the ordinary fee, given your *visage,* Addison. It's evident only the highest born and most well-off shall ever *see* your face, Addison, or indeed *know* of your existence in this house. Why, by the termination of seven years, you may have earned hundreds, indeed probably thousands of pounds."

It all sounded most promising, but I still didn't know what I would be doing and asked her once more.

"Well, it's rather an indelicate subject for a lady to

expatiate upon. But your friend shall do so. You do know, Mister MacIlhenny, don't you, that Bishop Huddlestone is scheduled to be here in a few minutes. Go to your regular chamber and prepare for him as usual. And while doing so, why not place our young friend in that side closet, the one with the grilled doorway, so he may see exactly how you have yourself fared so very well to date in my employ, and thus how it will be that his own fortune may soon be obtained."

"Come closer one brief moment, Addison," said she, and when I did, she took my hands—commenting "like a gentleman's"—and touched my cheeks, commenting, "like those of a babe in arms."

Lobster Tail took his leave of her, sulky, with a poor grace, shuffling his lanky body upstairs, and looking back to see if I was following.

"Catch him up, Addison," Athaliah Jukes advised. So I did, with alacrity. I could hear her counting coin upon the table below us.

We ascended to street level and then up one more, and only then did I make out how large the house was, especially its many doors to varied chambers on the top two landings. On each, some fellow lurked, and even by daylight, spermaceti oil might be sweetly smelt burning in the various lanterns ensconced upon the hallway walls.

From its stairways and corridors, the house appeared furnished very handsomely with a surfeit of furniture and furnishings both, whether pictures or marble busts upon plinths, and handsomely patterned papered walls. To tell the truth, I already liked this better than being about the docks in all weather.

More puzzling, however, than the many and various chambers, was that each such door held at eye level a brass plaque about the width of a man's hand and within it, in some fanciful design, the cursively detailed name of a single month of the year.

Lobster Tail entered into the second such—Taurus, April—and I followed.

Like the hallways, the chamber was well furnished and well warmed by a small fireplace. It contained a quite large bed, canopied over in olden style, with a commode at one end and a backless chair nearby. A window, small and high, provided a glimpse of the still inclement daylight out of doors.

"What shall you do here?"

"Receive a visitor," he said, surly. He then pointed to what appeared to be an adjoining closet, closed off by a wooden work grill. "In there goes yer fer the duration of my visit. Watch carefully and so yer copies whatever yer sees fer yer own edication," he added, pointing.

I entered the adjoining cabinet and found a small wooden stool where I myself would sit to witness what I guessed would be some kind of criminal activity, picking pockets, or lambasting, or who knows what? My mind was aflutter with so many exciting possibilities.

Before closing the fretted gate I asked, "Still, Lobs, you never said. Where is Tiger Jukes?"

"*She* is Tiger Jukes," he replied, looking downward from where we had just come. "The greedy b-tch down the stairs! Or hadn't yer figured it yet?"

Imagine then my surprise when Lobster—er, MacIlhenny—removed most of his clothing and lay himself upon his back upon the bedsheets.

Quickly enough, a timid knock on the door revealed his visitor, who stepped in, looking flushed and yet excited: a man of near sixty years of age, distinguished and even holy in both his mien and in his garb.

By this time, Lobster had taken up a small piece of reading

matter, a blue-paper-covered book no bigger than his hand, and he was perusing its pages, as though utterly unaware of any thing as common as a visitor.

And while he may have been unaware, one could not say the same for his member, so exposed within that expanse of reddish brown lawn, which immediately stood itself up taller. I imagined this visitor must be Bishop Huddlestone. He quietly as a mouse removed his coat—a large pale Ulster, against the wet—and he now bent down at one end of the bed as though in prayer. Covering his mouth, he tittered once, and then began to utter words difficult for me to ascertain, but which evidently Lobster Tail's member was familiar with, as it now erected itself to a great height as though some living object, and at the same time filled itself out sideways, too, flushing red, and all the while Lobster read on, making much of turning a page, and seemed unconscious of it or of his visitor.

Even from my impaired station, I could make out the Bishop's fingers reaching forward toward that large, increasingly ruddy object. But instead he satisfied himself with patting the surrounding hair and drawing the lightest of invisible lines upon the adjoining muscles and quite visible blue veins as though mapping out the territory. Quickly enough, the Bishop removed a silken scarf of the most blazing carmine dye from around his neck, and this he carefully arranged around Lobster's manhood, careful to enclose the paler orange sack. Was that Latin I heard Huddlestone uttering as he crept closer by inches to the desired object? Gingerly, as though expecting at any moment to be pushed away?

No sooner was the adored thing wrapped about and singled out than it must be oh-so-lightly stroked by quivering Bishopric fingertips until it grew quite red, upon which the still chanting Episcopal bent over and adjoined to those tips the pointed tip of his tongue. There it dandled and darted and made tiny little forays all over the now glistening object, which quite resembled a warrior's helmet, until it was fully widened and filled out.

Several minutes more of this finger and tongue play continued, Lobster all the while seemingly unaware and enthralled by his true-murder mystery story, until the Bishop could no longer resist and fell upon it all the way until a portion of it had quite disappeared into the maw of his priestly mouth. There the Bishop worked upon it, using hands, tongue, and mouth, all the time I swear muttering Latin homilies.

This went on for some time until suddenly, Lobster dropped his little booklet to one side, and using both largish hands, he held that sacred white-haired head until it was utterly still. The throat religious must still have been fully operational despite this ban, however. As I looked on, I noticed Mac's head suddenly fall backward, eyes up to the ceiling, and at the same time I saw his entire midsection, flat rear end and all, arise at least two inches off the bed sheets.

When he subsided back to them again a few minutes later, it was with the deepest exhalation, one from the very deepest part of him.

At this turn of events, the Bishop forbore from his ministrations, backed away slowly, unwrapped the scarf, sniffed it quickly, stuffed it into his waistcoat, then arose to stand, muttering more garbled Latin. Once he'd buttoned his trousers and his waistcoat, he made some kind of hand blessing over Lobster's supine body. Grasping his Ulster, he turned and rushed out.

Silence reigned in that chamber for the longest time.

Suddenly MacIlhenny rose up in bed and looked quickly at his member, which he dabbled at lightly with one finger.

"And so now, me Scallop-lad, yer have witnessed what 'tis that a house-lad does to earn his living."

I slipped out of hiding. "How many times *per diem*?"

"How many times per...whut?"

"Each day?"

"How many times could yer?"

"Three. Four. More," I assured him.

He looked at me more closely. "I took thee for a country lad in manners."

"Hardly so, old Lobs. I've been with a travelling theatre troupe. The Invincibles, man and maid, taught me quickly and fully enough how all this does pleasure a fellow within their caravans at nightfall."

"To have it done to yer?"

"Naturally. By maid *and* man. And also..." I teased.

"And also to do it yerself?" he then asked in some surprise. "For there, me Scallop Lad, lies the true earnings of this house-lad trade, though yer must never say so to the fat one down the stairs."

"Naturally, enough, Lobs, old fellow. To do so oneself is *all* the art. And in the theatre, one learns to *always* aim to please through art."

He took a while to absorb that information while he got dressed and tied on his shoes.

"Well, then, Scallop Lad," he said, arising now and beginning to put on his waistcoat. "I recognize that 'tis time fer me to seek another place. Or p'raps to retire from the field altogether."

"But why? Cannot we operate in tandem, or as a team?"

"Nay, Scallop, lad. With yer looks and yer experience, yer fortune is indeed here, as Tige fore-omened, inside this house. And upon fine, fat sausages and beefsteaks both shall yer dine!" he added. "Whilst I am, as yer've seen yerself, naught but a one-trick pony."

And though I tried to dissuade him, he would not listen,

and in a few days as I settled in, he left our criminal mistress's employ.

I asked Jem and the other house guards if they ever saw him about the docks, doing light-fingered work there, but they said no.

Yet another, a smooth faced scholar who paid well to merely kiss my pink and white bottom while he flogged his member, told me once that he believed my old compatriot had "gone the reformed whore's way." He swore that during the baptism of a well-off family where he'd accompanied his aged mother, he'd come upon MacIlhenny's inimitably lanky form clad in the ebony garb of a church deacon. He was silently presiding alongside higher Episcopals at one of our larger cathedrals. And so, I supposed, my friend had found a way in which to satisfy his *and* his client-Lord's inclinations.

❖

My days at Folly's Ditch working for Tiger Jukes lasted only seven months—seven memorable months admittedly—during which time Tiger became plumped up almost to bursting with the many cream-filled French desserts she ate. She was now able to keep a foreign pastry cook upon the premises as well as her regular chef, for she had more than a dozen to feed, inclusive of the four henchmen who guarded the house and the lads at all times who worked. During that same period, my own girth didn't alter an inch, but I certainly became more experienced in the more unusual manners of man—and eventually of woman too.

Mrs. Jukes had predicted great success for her establishment, and both she and I laboured diligently at ensuring that prediction came true. That first night I was taken to a room *en suite* on the top floor of the building, well away from the half-windowed, bottom-floor dormitory where McIlhenny and the other house-lads resided and slept whilst not at active duty. They were as regulated as though they were soldiers in training. From their nourishment four times per day, which was strictly regulated by their usual great hunger and inclination to be filled with various joints of meat, eggs, and cheese dishes—to the ten hours that they slept because ten was the minimum Tiger felt needed for "growing lads." To their "playtime" outside the house and, as a rule, at the open spaces down by the Overy docks themselves, where the boys' games and hijinks were overseen by two or three of those layabout Bravos that Addison had first encountered when entering the house.

This latter group of large, often muscular or simply stoutly powerful males had been promoted from their dock work and other less savoury occupations, and Addison was not surprised to discover four of them were related to the mistress. Jem and Calvin were cousins—German—while Gareth and Gwillyum were Welsh-born sons of a cousin of hers that she had ensorcelled into her business. The snub-nosed fellow who'd predicted I would "dine on fine Irish sausage" was named Michael Aloysius, and despite his marriage to the daughter of the "counting man," Anselm Harte Jukes, younger sibling of the deceased Mr. Jukes, Michael managed to impose his own fine Gaelic member into private chamber number six, my own new domain. Indeed, he did so often enough for the satisfaction of us both.

Michael A's. satisfaction because he was naturally hot-blooded, away from home a week at a time, and admittedly "taken some'at" with the newest lad. Or so I heard. This was a first for him, about which he received some good-natured larks from the other Bravos who were known to "dip into the wells of the Ditch" for their pleasure far more regularly than he.

And to my satisfaction as well, because after several odd and unsatisfying near-couplings in a day, there were times when I longed for a fellow who knew what he wanted and had no qualms about taking such, even if it meant a bit roughly.

The other encounters were often of the nature of the religious person with MacIlhenny, which was at least comprehensible. But quickly enough my presence became known in certain circles, and the carriage trade began to appear with some regularity in Rotherhithe Road. As a rule, these new clients' carriages were discreetly stabled nearby for no extra charge and their driver given an ale and chair upon which to catch up on his slumber while awaiting his master. In addition, individually owned and operated Hansom cabs began plying Rope Lane with greater frequency. Unoccupied, they would glide by at late hours, note a brightly lighted oil lamp signalling outside the double front door, and stop to pick up a fare that might have them traverse all the way to Greenwich or the Mayfair and beyond.

For that was how greatly the repute of my looks, demeanour, charm, and abilities soon travelled amongst those who would be interested in such. Meantime, I must meet with the other lads to discover what precisely I was expected to actually do, or if not do, then to receive. To my delight, I found the other lads to be pleased by my presence, and quite friendly. "Arter all, lad," Anthony (number four, Gemini) told me without any rancour at all, "the more fellers that crowd round to get at yer, the better the pickins for us'n, since to me knowledge yer cannot be at three places at one time. Agreed, lads?"

The others heartily agreed. More than that, they shared their experiences with me. "Now this Mr. Debingham, he's a rich and successful manufact'er. But what he likes most is to be undressed to his skivvies and be teased with little slaps and pinches. This excites him greatly and he'll show it. Meanwhile call him 'Bad Little Charles' and he'll grow greatly," affirmed Big Joe, the oldest of the lads (number ten, Capricorn). "If you then force yourself onto his face, he shall at first turn aside but done one more time he will then accept you greedily and soon also achieve his wet little happiness."

Slender, blond Freddy (number eight, The Scorpion) passed off his own well-to-do greengrocer. "Cover your pretties with a cloth, and prepare to be tongue-bathed, left ear to big right toe. For that is his demand. After that he'll gaze at yer while you slowly as possible flog yerself."

"I have known Greenie to deliver himself twice per session while gazing suchlike," Barney Digby (number seven, The Scales) added in.

But soon, high-toned strangers to the house appeared for whom none of the established lads had any previous knowledge. Tiger Jukes would receive morning and early afternoon cards wrapped in fine notepapers of crushed rag, even vellum, requesting "the pleasure of the company of Young Mr. Addison," often on a certain—usually that very—date, and a later time. As often as possible, she would accept the invitation. At the appointed time, the guest would be shown into Tiger's own drawing room decorated with much heavy mahogany furniture, the current style. After she had ascertained the guest's ability to pay and not to harm, she would ring a bell, and demure me would appear. After the second such visitor, she drove with me to Bond Street in her carriage for several fittings of clothing, so my appearance would be further appreciated. So particular in her directions for my shirts and suits was she that the tailors were certain we were son and doting mother.

I also appreciated how understated was my Mistress's transition from the initial three-person social encounter in her drawing room to a more intense two-person one. "Ah, time! It runs away for one so quickly!" Tiger would say, surprised by the striking of the clock that she herself had set an hour earlier. "I must attend to household matters. Please, Addison, dear, would you mind escorting the gentleman to your chamber and show him your wonderful drawings?" Or new sheets of music, or recently purchased lithograph, or whatever.

Once in chamber (number six, The Virgin), Mister So and So or Lord Such and Such would enfold me in his arms and kiss me as often and upon as many suddenly bared parts of my body as possible. I, meanwhile, would quietly labour to bring him to a final pleasure as rapidly as manually possible. Often my client would be surprised to arrive there, and a second effort would be required, by other more personal means, "only because you are such a great Lord." If I was interested enough, that would be even more delightfully achieved. A gift beyond what Tiger Jukes received would be forthcoming and a hope for a second or third or sixth meeting asked for. Once I'd delivered Lord Such and Such to the drawing room again and squeezed his hand in fond good-bye, there Anselm Jukes would be at his escritoire, beckoning a quick sit-down to inscribe a future appointment date.

None of the other lads were jealous, all of them looking outside to see the newest arrival and each one agreeing that "no such feller" ever visited them in their chambers. Eagerly did they ask me extremely personal questions about his conquests.

"His undergarments," Digby must know, "were they silken?"

To which I, who'd looked closely enough, replied, "Italian wool."

"Wool? Doesn't it itch?"

"Ah, Barney, wool so fine it's softer than silk."

Which would garner a satisfied, "Aah! I knew it."

But as I came to know the lads better, as well as their various boudoir attributes, I was able to pass some of my "better sort" on to them, especially if the lads had meanwhile developed "specialities."

For example, Anthony, who was rather exotic in looks, with his olive skin and Mediterranean features, was "jest natcherally happy to have a feller up me bum." So those who insisted upon such for me were treated to a double-lad experience, and while prettily I demurred, I also introduced Anthony, who would eagerly come in for the kill, as it were.

At times, Barney and or Big Joe might be gently called by a bell by the bed, all but invisible to guests, and join in with me and my client. The former for his acrobatic abilities—"I've never seen a nautical knot I couldn't imitate" was his motto. While Big Joe was another "prodigy of nature" genital wise, and eager to insert that prodigy into orifices one might think ordinarily too small for it.

Freddy, of course, was the codger specialist, a lad who became truly stimulated only when his client had snow white hair, moustache, and beard, although any two attributions would do. He satisfied these elders to such an extent that once they'd tasted his exquisites, they never asked for any other lad. It goes without saying he was more highly rewarded than any lad, except for myself, since this age group represented a most consistent class of visitors.

Meanwhile, the extra pelf gathered smoothly, and lust-stricken Michael Aloysius ensured its placement outside the house in a spot only he and I knew of. Four dozen sovereigns were in that hidey-hole when, one thundery evening, a new client made a quiet entrance into Folly's Ditch. Few of the men the lads were ever visited by were anyone but large, or full, or even plump gentlemen, since there was an assumed physical girth to anyone successful, and even the Peers were overfed by six-course repasts. So, the arrival of the slight and slender Eugene was notable. As was the fact that he was carefully, richly clothed and carried the proper accoutrements of a gentleman, from the rainbow hued pinfeather in his bowler hat down to tartan striped cross-strap for his boot spats. He had come particularly for Addison, he said, and Tiger had shrugged upon meeting him, meaning whatever Addison wished, yea or nay, before she would guide them into chamber six.

I was curious. This gentleman was unusually young—not quite beardless, he couldn't have reached the age of thirty. He was slight, supple, but apparently also strong and masterful, inured to getting his way. Leaving me even more curious.

Once we were alone, he asked me to undress, which I did slowly, and with as much erotic intent as possible. Eugene definitely showed signs of erotic interest. His cheeks and ears reddened, and his eyes shone. But he didn't for some minutes touch me, and, in fact, kept his hands to himself.

Disappointed that I wouldn't have even an athletic tussle with this new client but must perform solo for him, I tried to fantasize what a possible encounter might be, when of a sudden Eugene had me by my standing member, and muttering something or other unintelligible, made it clear that object was his main interest. I watched him during this operation, and there was a definite heightening of all of those outward manifestations of love-making. So, why was there nothing more? Was Eugene deprived of his own manhood? Was it inoperative? For the latter, more than one client depended upon one of Tiger's lads for successful stimulation to overcome such shortcomings.

I closed my eyes then, to think back upon Michael Aloysius's last visit, but when I opened my eyes a slit, I watched Eugene prodding himself through his trousers at— nothing at all. This is no fellow, I said to myself and extended a hand to remove Eugene's own and found unbuttoned exactly what one would expected to find with a Miss rather than a Mister. We quickly frigged each other to the expected bliss. Then, in a second, Eugene was up and about to leave.

"Wait!" I leapt up. When he insisted upon going, I said in a low voice, "Don't let me call Tiger's men on you for you to be thrashed."

Eugene turned with fear apparent.

"Why?" I said.

As she stuttered an unheard reply, I went on. "I care not who you are, 'sir.' I expect it is easier in this outfit to secure a cab and come a distance."

"Yes. You do understand."

"I do. You may visit whenever you wish, no matter what you may wear."

"You mean so long as the hag takes her majority cut of your wages?" Eugene said to my surprise.

"Said boldly enough. Does that mean you would offer me better business?"

"I could and would, if you would allow me to."

Her name was Vanessa, or so she said. She had been a young girl taken in hand by a glamorous elder and brought to the highest pitch of social acceptance in her own class, just one level below the highest Peers of the Realm. As such, she had succeeded in a fiduciary way well enough to retire.

"I travel incognito like this often," she said, "even among my own sort. I've heard your name spoken in several of the best clubs in the Mayfair. Why not take advantage of that repute you have gained and strike out on your own? I assume you have savings. A great deal more can be obtained. There are gentlemen who would not step so far out here to Southwark, even to gaze upon your lovely self. But should you be ensconced closer to Hyde Park, they could easily become a far more regular custom."

"And your own take would be?"

"A share of my own household expenses, nothing beyond."

But first I must see Vanessa, or Eugene as she preferred to be known, in action. And for that she must first invite me to a private party at such a club as Eugene had spoken of.

Getting out of the house under the best of circumstances would be a chore, Tiger guarded her cubs so carefully. However, I had heard there was an upcoming annual vacation to the seashore, which Tiger would not miss for anything, one to which she brought some of the older lads and a few of her Bravos. As a rule, the house at Folly's Ditch remained open for business, so long as the clients were known and, so to speak, established ones. No new ones might visit, since they must be greeted and first assessed by Mrs. Jukes's gimlet eyes. They had to be already quite familiarly recognizable to Jem or Michael Aloysius.

And so, Eugene visited, and I got myself out of the house via a back stairway. Once that so-called visit was over, Jem and Gwillyum heard Eugene thanking a lad who was not even present, as I'd already slipped out and was waiting in her carriage two doors down the street.

Her driver met her and dashed into Rotherwite Lane and then farther west. Just beyond the docks area, Eugene and I laughed and kissed each other quickly at such a successful lark. Not very long after, the sparkling wet landau was clattering over rain-washed Waterloo Bridge into central London.

I'd been to several upper-class emporia, thanks to Tiger's insistence that I dress higher than my station, but even so, the club we entered together took me by surprise. Not that it was ornate—it was anything but. Rather because it was so settled, so there, really, in all its dark wood wainscoting and deep tufted leather arm-chaired glory. Not a single object was small, thin, or in any way other than the steadiest and stoutest of its kind.

This particular get-together was a punch and smoking party, Eugene told me. I didn't smoke cigars and hadn't liked the one I'd once tried. But I found that with the windows and French doors open to a sort of second-storey stone terrazzo, I could breathe easily enough through the cigar and cigaret fumes. She had dressed me in my best clothing with a few of her own accessories, and the single glance I caught of us in a floor to ceiling looking glass as we were coming up to the second floor corridor showed me a fellow even I was amazed to see.

Not everyone knew Addison by name or reputation. Possibly none did. That was fine. I would be relaxed and confident and pass as one of the fellows. Meanwhile as I looked about myself, I saw at least one other person *en travesti*, taller, older, with a deeper voice and bewildering confidence, even swagger.

"I see you've noticed Terence," a voice said next to my left ear. "Quite a remarkable story there."

The speaker was a tall, *soigne*, ginger-haired fellow with nearly crimson moustache and a perfectly tonsured matching shovel beard. He'd been among a group Eugene had introduced, and I had noted these features immediately as well as his bright, sometimes hazel but more often green as a dragonfly, eyes.

"Indeed! I take it that you, Lord Tay, shall be kind enough to excuse my current ignorance and impart that story?"

The ginger eyebrows danced over the now merry green eyes.

"'Tis completely physiological in nature," Tay said in a low voice.

"Completely?"

"Fearfully so. An undescended—" Here he leaned in close and slid a large hand along my inseam. "Testicle!"

He had found my own double number of that organ, and his hand must be rather delicately lifted away.

So, that was the story that Terence was giving out! Well, why not?

"Fearful, of course," I commented, "to those of us who are fortunately fully descended." Here I took hold of Tay's inseam and found my mark.

"Touché!" Tay said, holding my hand in place. "Now that we are properly introduced and identified, more punch?" he offered with the other.

Eugene arrived with Terence and some other actual gentlemen to be introduced and Lord Tay slipped away. Throughout the next half hour or so until my group adjourned to a late supper of cold meats and cheese in a lower hall, I kept an eye on Tay, who never seemed to be too far away from us.

"Your companion?" he queried. "Is he as much for the ladies as I have heard?"

"What have you heard?"

"Two fellows I know well witnessed Eugene with a chambermaid, not fully hidden from view, and they watched him pleasure the lass with his hand until she became so loud he needed his other hand to gag her and then she nearly fainted."

That was interesting.

"And I've heard report that he is an expert in the French manner," Tay continued, rubbing his tongue along his upper lips.

"While I've not myself witnessed Eugene engaged with any maid," I said, "nevertheless, I'm left in no doubt of Eugene's many oral talents."

"*Many* oral talents! Do you mean to say…?" But then he

was called away by insistent friends whom he'd promised to join for supper outside the club.

When we were again in the carriage and headed back south of the Thames, Vanessa asked, "What did Laurence want of you?"

"Laurence? You mean Lord Tay?"

She nodded.

"He wanted to see if I had both of my balls."

"Because you were the prettiest there," Vanessa assured him. "So, he wanted to be certain which you were," and as she spoke she made her own inspection, busily opening my trouser buttons.

"Odd. I thought you were the prettiest," I said as she worked to bring me off. But I was thinking of Laurence, Lord Tay, all the time she was frigging us together.

❖

One more such adventure was needed so that those in the house who may or may not have noticed me gone a while or returned would pass it off as a lark or at least not feel uncomfortable with the situation. This one took place at the end of that fortnight, and Eugene and I took a larger, faster four-horse brougham than usual, not into town but somewhat south and east to what I was told was a house party.

Such an event had become increasingly common among Eugene's set, she told me, and was often written up in society pages the following week. Unlike the jolly-fellow-well-met atmosphere of the supposedly all-male club party, this was a display of both genders, and also a display of wealth although displayed mostly to one's own equals, perhaps to a few poor relations and other hangers-on—and, of course, to the staff, which often numbered in the scores.

These country manses were mostly newly built, financed by recent, successful business schemes and fresh-as-paint affluence and were quite large, consisting of a dozen public indoor and semi-outdoor rooms as well as at least a score of bed chambers for guests. Games and sports were played out on the lawns and courts as well as indoor games in chambers specifically built for billiards or snooker. Bridge, whist, and other popular card games were common. Two younger fellows sharing a room was also common and younger fellows were requested, indeed absolutely required, since for many a Mama, house parties were the *ne plus ultra* crux of their marriage plans for their well brought up and substantial, if seldom beautiful, daughters.

One might encounter young men in such numbers of such breeding and so very casually at house parties, so that the beginning of the Season In-Town sometime in mid-October was deemed do-or-die in the annual upper crust British mating game. Eugene flirted outrageously with several heiresses, including an American named Rosemary. And though I kept my eyes on lookout, I never found her with a chambermaid, unless she was better hidden than before.

Instead I looked around more circumspectly and most particularly at those young men who remained unattached after several rounds at court tennis or whist. I even more noticed those who appeared to be making what were clearly financial engagements leading to marriages where they might ensure that they later remained free enough for other types of more personal pleasure. These, I thought, might become the basis of my own future clientele.

Not exactly among this set was Laurence, Lord Tay, who was already in residence at Gathering Oaks, as this monstrosity of a house was known, when Eugene and I arrived for luncheon. He may have already been in residence for a period of time, since the owners, Prescott-Tays, were relatives. He clearly had several girls and especially their Mamas chasing after him. But his elusiveness was legendary, abetted by the story put about that he had been engaged to a lovely if fragile Yorkshire Miss, possessor of a manufacturing fortune, who had foolishly acquired a nasty ague and, even more absurdly, had died of it during their long engagement. As a result, Laurence was deemed "sensitive," and even "rather morbid."

"You, of course, are too young for any such course of action, are you not, Mr. Addison?" a particularly simpering Mama asked, as we estivated in wickerwork swings upon a veranda, while her bored daughter looked elsewhere in embarrassment. "Yes, of course, too young," the Mama answered herself.

"But Lord Tay," I asked her. "He's of the right age, is he not?"

"The perfect age."

"I don't like him, Mama," her daughter put in. "He's sarcastic."

"Well, maybe a little," her Mama allowed.

"Surely," I interrupted, "he can't be much of a Lord, can he? I mean, where are his lands exactly?"

"Scotland," both women replied, their research deep and complete. "Along the river Tay, I believe," Mama added. "That would mean quite a lot of land."

That didn't sound quite correct to me. "Perhaps, but what do they grow there? Oats? Barley? Rye? None of those are high yielding crops."

"It's probably all rotten," the girl said, "You know, a lot of subsistence farmers who can barely pay rents."

"That can't amount to very much, can it?"

"It adds up," phlegmatic Mama insisted. "And anyway, one doesn't marry a Lord for *his* money."

"One doesn't?"

"Of course not." Her daughter spelled out the life-lesson. "One *has* the money *and then* marries the Lord. It would be completely unfair if he were landed, beautiful, sardonic, *and* rich. What could a girl bring to the table?"

"Well put, Gwen," her mother agreed.

Somewhat later, before Eugene called me to depart, I found myself playing croquet in a triples team, against the same mother-daughter duo and the Lord.

"Beware those ladies," I warned Tay under his breath.

"Not to worry. They've long ago given up on me," he said, adding, "Shall we go for a ride on the downs? My cousin's stable isn't at all bad, and we might be alone."

That's when Eugene showed up, and I promptly said my good-byes.

This second time I was illegally outside the House, going home was a longer journey. Before she rifled my trousers, Vanessa asked what I had learned.

"A very great deal," I replied and told her some of it.

"Very good," she agreed. "And who do you think asked me particularly about your whereabouts this coming fortnight?"

I liked guessing games and turned out to be good at this one. "Lord Afton's son, Ralph. That half-German Baron something or other, Rolf-Heinz. And that arms manufacturer's heir, what's his name, don't tell me—Billingham?"

"Only three?"

"Well, then, a wild guess, also that nephew of Mrs. Prescott-Tay, that Nigel King fellow?"

"Two others, also. But those three are enough for a start once you are on your own again."

"Lord Tay asked me to ride with him," I reported. "Would he be number six?"

She didn't answer then nor later.

We reached the house not an hour before Mrs. Jukes made her own, more ballyhooed, return. By then I was alone again, counting my earnings.

Tiger had rested sufficiently during the fortnight vacation by the sea that her next levee was less of an interrogation of the lads than usual. Instead, she was gracious, she passed out sweets and even discreet little parcels of praise. Clearly, she had looked at the carefully noted record books of her dull young in-law and knew to a penny what earnings had come in.

"It does a lady's soul good to know that the youth she has worked so assiduously to help in this world have seen fit to recompense that nourishment," she said generally, before particularising each of the six who had remained behind. Those each received an appropriate compliment, especially Big Joe and myself, who "surpassed expectations and seems to have brought in a profitable new client."

"How long I can keep that new client is the question."

"Is there a problem one should know of?" Tiger asked.

"The profitable new client dislikes coming all the way here."

This wasn't the first time Tiger had heard this complaint from a lad. She dove into the record book and noted, "Five times in a fortnight. Perhaps an exception could be made if the client sent his own carriage. Is that within the realm of possibility, dear?" I knew this would mean no extra cost for her for Hansom cab fees.

"That was the very offer made," I said as diffidently as possible.

"And the client is comfortable?" Tiger asked.

"Comfortable enough, Mrs. Jukes."

"Good. Then we'll send a card informing him. Perhaps a day before his next promised visit? Anselm, you will see to that."

And her levee continued.

And so the scene was set and the plan moved forward, slowly, so as to not cause unnecessary alarm, and in a regulated and stately manner, so that even one small deviation would eventually be accepted. That required another five visits to Eugene by his own carriage, until on the fifth such visit, I not only invoked that deviation by staying out overnight, but simply did not return. Moreover, by the time I was missed at one of Tiger Juke's morning business levees, I was already at Portsmouth Harbour, *en travesti* as the doubly veiled and somewhat ailing lady known as "Mrs. V. LaBenthe" traveling *en suite* with Mr. Eugene LaBenthe—Vanessa—and their two servants by packet across the channel to Dieppe.

Naturally Tiger's man, Michael Aloysius, felt betrayed by this signal turn of events, but well aware of the extremely high temper this would cause in the already volcanic Mrs. Jukes, he dared not say a word of our relations. Nor for a longish time dared he look into that place where he had been helping me stash my earnings. This was a Thameside private postal office that also sold weekly subscriptions to the Metropolitan Transit Line and the omnibus service newly installed in various newer areas of the city. When he did dare try the key to the safety box, he was pleasantly surprised it opened to a note: *My best lover ever—I shall miss you dearly* and enough sovereigns to keep his mouth shut for the near future at least.

In truth, it was enough that when the clerk-owner of the postal establishment asked if Michael Aloysius was looking for a position, he answered in the affirmative. Despite his relational connection to Folly's Ditch, he soon convinced his wife to relocate to Lambeth, where he eventually opened his own version of that postal and omnibus office. Those profits allowed a greater scope to *her* own social ambition, and far better opportunities for shopping. Years later, a substantial woman herself, she would look back at Folly's Ditch as "that rather dark period of our youth." Cleverly, she never once asked Michael Aloysius where he discovered or how he had come about this life-changing treasure.

The Tiger raged and tore about for some weeks denouncing me, then came to her senses and all was as before. The other lads were still occupied, and a few, like Digby, had grown into their young manhood with surprisingly solidified good looks. With a little pampering and the right outfitting, he might easily ascend into my former chamber, number six, off the drawing room, and call himself Addison to new clients seeking that boy-paragon.

This paragon returned from the Continent to —— Street, taking up residence as planned in those rooms in the edifice semi-attached to Eugene's. There, in a matter of weeks, I managed to communicate to those of my previous clients who I still wished to see, and slowly, but with a sure hand—Eugene's hand for the most part—I amassed a superior clientele, one we had together first envisaged at Gathering Oaks.

It was composed of eligible young men who seemed eternally eligible and their newly-wed acquaintances who found that marrying into wealth allowed them more than enough free time to spend long hours at their club, and eventually, nearby, in my chambers. Nor were more punch and cigar nights at selected clubs exempt. And, of course, house-parties in Sussex and Kent remained a rich field for discovering new clients among the disenchanted and the sensually uncertain. Late night and early morning invasions of their bedrooms by a lost Addison soon discovered which of them were ripe to become regulars.

Lord Tay, "Laurence," was a recurrent, one might almost say persistent staple of the latter social gatherings, if an increasingly enigmatic one. He certainly had prime opportunities for furthering his fortune. One young lady from Ohio combined blue eyes and brunette hair, taste, excellent equestrian abilities, the usual ladylike accomplishments, and an enormous endowment. Furthermore, she preferred England and Scotland to America and adored the lean and satiric fellow despite his facial hair. But by the end of that season, he still hadn't made a move, and she was taken by another—one of my irregular clients who excused his increasingly sporadic visits thereafter by saying, "Difficult to admit as it is, I'm coming to really like my wife. These American girls are so fresh!" Despite that, neither Eugene nor any of his informants could find a "Greek taint" to the curious Scottish Lord, even after a long search.

Intriguingly, one of those house parties yielded a literary personage who became very interested in Eugene while there and was so fascinated by what he discovered that he offered *entrée* to a loftier sort of club for both Eugene and me.

Xavier Quentin Pell was a very minor poet. Yet because he'd been an Apostle at University, he hadn't very far to go to have all the connexions a very minor poet of his day and place might require to make his mark. He certainly never had any fiduciary necessity for advancement, being a child of fortune of his time with "intrusted" railroad share dividends to burn. Nor—frankly—had he even a quivering of the aspiration to rise into becoming a Tennyson, a Browning, or even a Swinburne.

But an eccentric Mathematics professor and sometime bedmate-friend of Pell's at school, named Mr. Dodgson, held a certain unstinting regard for him; Mrs. Meredith giggled when she allowed she simply had to have Pell at her Sunday repasts; the Ruskins insisted he miss far fewer of their intellectual teas than he already had. Besides, being so civil and lightly witty and well spoken, he was so pleasant to look upon, that even I had to admit Pell certainly boded well for a well-bred Englishman at the advanced age of thirty-and-one in the final decades of the nineteenth century.

Ex-Queue, as I quickly came to term him in sobriquet, became a charming addendum to our Addison-Eugene nexus, both socially and in the bedroom. It took Pell some time to understand why Eugene never undressed completely, but then it didn't really matter to him, since he was as well taken care of as he took care of his *amore*. He considerably extended our social network, and I began pondering hiring a secretary or some sort of clerk, perhaps only in the mornings, to keep my visiting schedule more tightly in place. I even lackadaisically interviewed one or two apparently down on their luck young fellows who'd had experience in some lesser capacity as clerks, and who clearly seemed daunted by these new surroundings.

It was only when the third lad to show up almost silently admitted he had family in Brick Lane and knew of the Villas Sheen that I really perked up.

The boy was about thirteen or fourteen years of age, and his hands were chapped enough to signify that he had been engaged in manual and not very clean labour for several years. Despite that, he was personally neat and trim, his murkily dark hair was not left uncut overlong, his head and face displayed what Ex-Queue would term "an honest British yeoman."

"What's needed here," I told the interviewee, "is someone who can read and write and keep dates and times in a book, who is also willing to be of general use. Someone who might hail a Hansom, or pre-arrange a carriage, someone who could receive important communications and deliver the same."

"I believe I can do all that, sir."

"Often I am visited by gentlemen of high station," I

appended, liking how alertly the lad had spoken up. "My lad must keep everything he sees and hears to himself."

"I have well learned discretion already, sir. Must where I was brought up."

I supposed that was so. "You would reside here in the floor below, in a chamber next to those of my friend and neighbour's manservant and his wife, who is our general cook. She has a female cousin who serves as char for both of our residences. They would provide you with meals and bed linens. They too are unusually discreet, and well paid—as you would be. You might take time off to visit your family, when you are not needed. For example, if I travel to a country residence of my familiars and you should wish to accompany me in those cases, you would be taken care of as usual, along with their own servants."

The lad looked intelligent and eager, so I dropped a week of visiting cards I'd received and had hastily noted myself with coming appointments and handed the lad pen and ink and paper.

"Can you read my handwriting? Good, then arrange these correctly for date and time of appointment."

I stepped to the window, so as to not oversee the lad. But the window was shadowed so that I might see by reflection. I was pleased to see the lad roll back his jacket arms and shirtsleeves and then tear off a deckled edge of the paper as an ink-guard. In less than ten minutes, he had arranged the dates and times in a completely regular fashion.

"Very good," I admitted. "You are neat, too. But I will provide a small record book for you to write in. You are to date each page appropriately whenever an appointment comes in and to ensure that they do not overlap. Every morning, when I ask for my tea, you will also bring the day's appointments."

"Might I ask," the lad pointed to an entry, "what it signifies when there is an Ex and then Queue, like this?"

"That is a friend. Did you also notice two dashes after a name or initials? That means my appointment is not here but outside this flat, and that a Hansom or carriage is needed and ought to be readied a half hour to an hour beforehand."

The lad ventured a shy smile. All this was within his capability.

"Your clothing is clean but not new. I'll bring you to an emporium where you will try on two sets of ready-made suit and shirts and etcetera to wear in my service." I quickly wrote at the bottom of the page an amount of money.

"Is this agreeable as a wage?"

"Yes, sir."

"If you do well, it could rise. And if you are good and discreet, my friends might even tip you. Will your family need to see you oftener than I've allowed?"

"Not if I'm in good service, like this, sir."

"What is your name?"

"Thomas, sir. Thom Cullen."

"Well, Thom Cullen, you are hired on to be my man. Now go downstairs, find your way to the servants there, and fetch me tea and crumpet. And when you have brought it, have both of those for yourself down there."

"Yes, sir," said Thom Cullen, as happy to be fed as to be taken on. He half bowed as he left.

There was a moment when I thought: that could have been myself, or my brother Tom some years ago. But that melancholy moment passed.

"Damn me!" I said aloud when I was alone. "I have just turned seventeen years of age, and I am in business and have myself a manservant."

❖

It was Ex-Queue who suggested it. As a prank, he said. It was one of those larks that Pell always came up with after all three of us had pleasured ourselves and each other and were lying about smoking cigarets. Those "fantastickal conceits" often came and went without any issue. This time, however, Vanessa took it up quickly, because as she put it, "Laurence certainly has *something* coming to him." The poet had explained that he had it on the best authority Lord Tay had actually attended one of those "séance-table-knocking things," in the hopes of attaining communication with the defunct heiress he was always going on about.

"With what result?" she asked.

"None."

"How very disappointing."

"Yes. Perhaps we should be more productive. We ought to produce her for him," Ex-Queue said in no uncertain terms, and Vanessa seconded it.

How this was to be done was a weightier question. Knockings and mists were one thing. Producing a memorable event was quite another, and when we three spoke of it, a memorable event was what we believed we must produce.

"Thom Cullen dressed as the Yorkshire Miss?" I suggested.

"Myself dressed as the Yorkshire Miss," Vanessa replied. "Laurence has never seen me out of men's clothing and has no idea."

"We surely can find a roto of the lass from her local newspaper's obituary and make you up to resemble her," Ex-Queue said. "Perhaps a garment or decoration similar to hers would add verisimilitude. Sheets otherwise."

"She will have to be at a distance from the séance table, yet visible," I opined. "Perhaps in an alcove, nook, or on a dais or…"

"We'd have to do it elsewhere. Nowhere near any of our addresses."

"There's a small Odeon closed for years that I know of on property mired in contending lawsuits in Chancery," Pell said. "I don't doubt we could rent it for a night at a low rate. It possesses such an alcove."

"You may have to be the Swami," Vanessa said to me. "Can you do a proper foreign accent?"

"Yaass, my deeaaah. I cawn," I replied, remembering how the woman at the onion and mangel stall in Covent Garden spoke. She was, I believed, Herzegovinian. Or Venezuelan. One or the other.

After the third discussion, we agreed to do it. The place was rented for two nights. The first for a rather technical go-through: a mist machine and coloured stage lights were borrowed from the theatre itself. Two sets of draperies were hung thickly, taken from the theatre's own storage.

We used the chapel-like extension of the original inner lobby, which contained such an alcove. It was originally the tea shop of the place, where theatre-goers might imbibe during the interval. Draped, it made for an intimate space. Naturally, it contained an alcove in front of a stairway. A statue of Erato, probably in the belief that any muse would serve for theatre, was placed on a four-foot stone plinth. The alcove was to be doubly draped. Vanessa would have to move to and from the plinth, covering the statue with drapes and herself be the focus of attention. A cord from those drapes was prepared and nailed in place under a deal table so that I could pull the drapes slowly open and then closed.

One question was whether Thom Cullen would agree to

be a participant in the pantomime. When asked, he did agree, with jollity and gusto. As did Vanessa's own two servants, sober to the point of dourness, who agreed to impersonate other clients who had lost their own loved ones and wished to see them again. They would be dressed in portions of Pell and Vanessa's cast-off clothing.

That night, I attended upon Lord Tay and Pell at their club and seconded Pell's contention that genuine materializations had occurred at such séances. "I am myself too frightened of such horrors," I said with a shudder, "but I will go with you in the cab to the door, and leave you at the place." In reality, I would get out on the next street, and slip back into the building to play my role.

After some demurral, Laurence's excitement was palpable.

The other two attendees were already in place there, funereal in garb and aspect. They merely nodded to Pell and Tay's greeting. A sober Thom Cullen, dressed in his usual suit but with black armbands and a dark turban upon his head wrapped by Vanessa, led the four into the heavily draped chamber. He seated them so that Lord Tay would face the alcove with the author on one side and myself as Swami on the other. The clients as well as Cullen would complete the circle. The alcove itself was semi draped, the statue of Erato in deep shadow.

As they placed themselves around the circular table, I arrived, soot and blacking upon my nose, chin, and forehead, a pair of blue-glass spectacles in front of my eyes, and another turban about my head. My costume consisted of more drapery that Vanessa had wrapped around my slender form, cinched with a gaudy gold cloth belt.

They were enjoined to all hold hands. "Once the circle is established," I began in an accent that would waver all night, but never be fully comprehensible as one nationality or another, "it must not be broken until I say so. This is well understood, yes?"

All agreed. Silence ensued, and then I began low-voiced chanting. At one point, Vanessa took up the chanting in a barely audible voice from her spot behind the drapes in the alcove.

Not to be fazed, I intoned, "Heed! My spirit guide Althea is here."

The first spirit to make an aural appearance, thanks to Vanessa's lowest tone of voice, was a gentleman named Anthony Parduc, "late of the shire of St. Albans," who asked Thom Cullen if he had located his "long-missing traveling shave-kit in a tooled leather container." His response had been prepared.

Cullen answered, "But where shall I look for it?"

"Under the watch case of mine you secreted upon your person moments before you announced my departure from this earth." This was not the prepared answer, and Thom sputtered and wasn't able to reply. This was sufficiently realistic for Laurence to be impressed.

Next came a childish voice which the butler replied to, asking, "Is that you, Maisie?" Maisie said it was and to his consternation predicted he would be joining her soon, and they would play games as they used to do. "You recall, dear uncle, the ones with my skirts up and covering my face." That rather stopped him from any more questions.

Another longish silence ensued, and then Thomas released agreed-upon mist from beneath his chair, to cover over the alcove drapes and then reveal them opened. I as Swami announced, "A very strong presence has entered this chamber. My Althea says she is powerless to resist its baleful influence. She is going and—ah!" Suddenly the alcove was undraped and Vanessa as the Yorkshire Miss could be ascertained upon the plinth yet as though floating in the mist.

Here a bit of luck was added to the evening. Not two days earlier, while looking through the photographic plates of a professional he knew, Pell had come upon one of Lord Tay and his brothers. One was distinctly thin, almost to the point of starvation, obviously quite ill. When Pell asked a friend in the club that evening, he was told the brother had since died. His name was Afton.

Vanessa was saying in a soft voice, "Afton, Afton, Afton, come back, come back, fear me not. For I am more than a sister to you." She repeated this until it was loud and clear enough to be heard.

"Oh, God. Are they together even now?" Lord Tay shouted, and kicked the chair from under himself as he attempted to rise. He had been carefully placed, however, and he could not get away from my own tightly gripped fist on one side and Pell's on the other. Both of us struggled while enjoining him to not break the circle no matter what he did.

"Afton. Afton, wait for me!" Vanessa moaned in a dying voice, then the mist returned, and Laurence slumped over the table. Soon enough the drapes were fully shut over the alcove, and I called an end to the séance.

Released, Lord Tay leapt up and rushed into the alcove only to find the statue of Erato there.

"Why so agitated?" Pell asked. Laurence turned to him with agony written upon his face. "I stole her from Afton in life. I told her he could never be well enough to be a husband and father. And now they spite me in death by being together!"

❖

Distraught he may have been, but Lord Tay ended up serving me very well indeed. Word of that sensational communication with spirits led to several members of the club, and indeed Laurence himself, begging for another such opportunity to commune.

We conspirators naturally felt vindicated. I found myself thinking this might be a lucrative and less physically demanding manner of earning my keep and it might be a bit more distinguished, once I thought about it. I was seventeen years old, nearly a grown man, and I'd experienced a great deal that London and its environs might offer the ambitious, intelligent, otherwise indigent lad. Even so, I must acknowledge that problems existed with repeating, never mind expanding, that first séance as or more successfully.

One of these was almost immediately solved when Thom Cullen revealed he was chums with the messenger lad of the employment bureau that had in fact sent him to me for work, an agency that supplied service to the best families in London town.

"Meaning what, exactly," I asked.

"Meaning sir, I have an in on private information."

"An in on whom?"

"Well, sir," Thom Cullen said, pulling out the little bound notebook of foolscap I had given him the first day he'd been hired and rattling off a dozen names. "Will any of those do?"

"I believe so. Yes, indeed."

I promptly raised the lad's wages.

The following day I met Ex-Queue at the club and showed him the list, suggesting that we expand our field of spiritism.

"Who is this fellow, then?" Meaning Cullen's friend. "Not one of those for-hire detective fellows?" he asked. He'd been thinking about the subject after rereading Wilkie Collins's novel *The Moonstone,* and he thought this private detection business was an idea worth looking into further to write up and possibly even work up into some sort of story for the magazines.

"He's merely a messenger, although a very well-connected one. Hardly a for-hire detective, although my own lad seems to have a talent for the work."

"Anything at all subversive is exactly up his line, eh?" Pell asked smarmily. Before I could answer, he pointed to the list. "These two names and perhaps this name here."

"As I'd hoped."

"But you understand that expanding this sort of thing would go well beyond merely a lark or two."

"I'm well aware of the fact, Mr. Pell."

"It will require time, planning, and something of an outlay of expenditure."

"Again, I concur, Mr. Pell. But with Lord Tay as good as a shill for us already," I pointed out, "advance promotion would be the least of our expenses."

"At least one rather large handyman would be required," Pell said. "For heavy lifting and other sundry activities."

"For security purposes also. Yes, I think I know just the fellow, Mr. Pell." I was thinking of Michael Aloysius, whom I'd spotted outside his Lambeth Private Postal Clerkship while passing in a cab.

Surprisingly, while she thought the idea both "barmy and beautiful," Vanessa begged off, citing her all-encompassing new interest in equestrian activities. Someone or other at a house party had gotten her enthusiastic over Arabian bred stallions, and she'd gone into it, as with most things in her life, head over heels. Me and Pell scarcely saw her for our bi-weekly games in my chambers. But when asked about the séance business, she said she might allow herself to be drawn back at least one more time, if it meant with Laurence, Lord Tay himself, for whom she admitted she possessed a soft spot.

That final bedside romp trio took place in her own rooms,

with a somewhat inebriated, although by no means limp, Scots peer, an ardent me busily undressing him, and once that had been accomplished, Eugene appeared and unbuttoned what lay beneath his trousers for Laurence's surprise and delectation. Tay was just sober enough to enjoy both youth and lady. When he was placed inside a cab and sent home some hours later, he declared, "I shall return," to their amusement.

But before he could deliver on that promise, he fulfilled my prediction and delivered new clients for the séances. Nor was he above adding information of a rather intimate quality beyond even what Thom Cullen and his confederate might discover to aid in our productions.

Those two hireling youths became the leading behind-the-scenes practitioners of the séances, while Michael Aloysius—eager to gain additional income as well as regain a spot in my own bedchamber, came up with new and often unusual methods of producing the spiritualist evenings. For an example, he had laboured for a musical supply depot for some months while still a lad, and so he introduced various horns and pipes and organs which might be hidden off-stage, as it were, to emit eerie sounds, moans, groans, and even passable animal mewls as needed.

But then Pell himself became more often indisposed or otherwise occupied with various dinners and salons he decreed he simply must attend. No matter. He was no longer absolutely required. Of course, that also meant the financial take from each séance was no longer divided but single, except payouts to those hired. Even so, I found that one of these performances a week produced enough income that I now need accept fewer visitors for my other type of employment, and from an even smaller and even more select company of gentlemen.

After a while, Lord Tay stopped coming, too. In the club,

it was being bruited about that he and Eugene were now the fastest of friends and boon riding companions, spending increasing amounts of time together.

Pell's newest—and slimmest—volume of verse was published and achieved an astonishing groundswell of positive reviews. That meant increased sales, and a second and then third printing was ordered. No one could be more astonished, nor more grateful than Ex-Queue himself!

After several more months. it all seemed so flowing, so easy, that it couldn't last—and it didn't.

❖

"Where, lad, is my tea?"
"There is none." The lad was completely confused.
"Then ask Cook for some."
"Cook isn't there. Butler neither. The fire on the hob is out. No one is to be seen in their rooms neither," Cullen reported. "I thought it oddly quiet when I woke, although they are never noisy folk."

I wrapped my robe more tightly around myself and, taking Thom by the hand, walked him down the stairs to the chambers below.

Vacant, as reported. Without a fire, as reported. All three chambers, including the servants' bed and sitting chambers empty, their wardrobe closets empty of clothing. All of it clean enough but bereft of human—even of feline—company. That was perplexing enough.

"No word at all of them leaving?" I asked.
"None to myself, sir," Cullen reported.
"Nor to myself. And the cupboards are equally bereft of food."

"Shall I go down and out to the Widow's Mite," he said, naming a local public house we sometimes utilized at odd hours, "for tea and toast, sir?"

"Why don't you?" I handed him some coins from my robe pockets.

While Thom did that, I went back upstairs and dressed for the street. I then descended and knocked on Vanessa's front door. And waited. And knocked. And waited. When no one came to open it, I went back to the street, opened the gate there, dropped three steps down to the service entry, and knocked at that door. Also to no avail. Looking in the windows there as best as I might, I was greeted by what seemed to be unoccupied servants' and kitchen rooms. It was as though Vanessa, her servants, and her entire household had overnight removed themselves to another location entirely, without word, without warning, with never a fare-thee-well.

We ate breakfast, master and man, together, hungrily, yet in a state of much perplexity. I'd given Thomas enough coins for a larger repast: rashers of bacon, parboiled eggs in little cups, a heap of toasted bread with pots of butter and jams, as well as a substantial metal pot of strongly brewed tea. We ate, we drank with appetite, and between mouthfuls, we two chewed over the mystery. We had been at the little theatre for a séance and as usual had arrived home quite late the previous evening, and all had been—as usual—dark when we came in quietly.

I started up and went to my bedchamber and jacket. Sure enough, the pay for the evening's entertainment was intact. Some more recent of my savings were in a drawer of the large wardrobe in his room. But the bulk of it had been placed for security in a wall safe in Vanessa's own bedchamber. If no one else returned there, I would have to find a way in and pry it open. If it was even there?

"It's gone!" I said, thinking aloud. "It must be, all of it. With them."

"Sir?"

Just then we heard a loud knocking at the door two floors below. Thom leapt up to go answer it.

"Wait." I pulled him back and went to a small window from which we might look out and down without being seen.

Two stout men, and with them a bobby. What in the world?

"Bailiffs, sir!" Thom said, pulling me back in. "I've seen their kind before. They have come to evict or arrest or both. Shall I go let them in?"

"No. Follow me." I dragged Thomas into my bedchamber, pulled out a travel case, and began tossing in my best clothing, leaving some still hanging by a shoulder or sleeve. I then filled up a smaller case with my personal effects. My money I kept upon my person. Below, the knocking was added to by shouting of an intemperate nature. "Climb out back here," I directed Thom, "and get to the rooftop with all this, and cross over until you are well away from these buildings."

"But, sir, what about you? They'll take you in."

"We'll see about that. Go now, and we'll meet at the back door of the news-seller's stall. Go, now."

I then hid the breakfast remnants in a cupboard, ruffled my clothing and hair, and went down to answer the door.

"It's about damned time," one fat elderly man declared.

"'Twas sleeping," I said with as much of a Villa Sheen accent as I could recall.

"We are bailiffs of the law, and we have a writ here to come demand payment," the other stout fellow thundered as they pushed past me and began up the stairs.

"Master's asleep, he is!"

"Not for long, he isn't," the second fat one shouted. "Awake! Awake up there!"

I had intended to slip out past them, but the constable remained at the doorway and looked at me as though daring me to try it.

"Get upstairs and help them fetch your master!"

I went up slowly and with a poor grace, in time to see the bailiffs take a look around the servants' quarters.

"Not a soul," one thundered. "Not even a fire lit."

"Whose chamber is this?" the other thundered. It was Thom Cullens's bed chamber.

"Mine, sir. You just woke me from sleep from here. Shall I go fetch my master for you?"

"You remain here," one said to him. "I've got a bad feeling about this, Bill," he said to his companion in a lower voice.

"Aye. Me too, Burt," the other said angrily. He pushed me into Cullen's bedchamber and attempted to lock the door behind him. But the lock was broken, so he wedged a stick in there instead.

I gathered up as many of Thomas's few belongings as I could, wrapped them inside an overcoat, and wrapped all that about with a tightened belt. I opened the single little window from his bedchamber and dropped the bundle onto a jutting rooftop. It wouldn't be difficult to climb up and retrieve it later on. I then dressed himself in what outer clothing and cap remained to aid my disguise as servant lad, and sat waiting, until I heard their shouting and thundering steps back down to my floor, where they thrust open the door. "He's skipped. He's made a run for it, that rum master of yours! Where's he gone to?"

"What? Who? Where? Isn't he upstairs?"

"Damn you, he is not!" one declared.

"He's made a run for it. Skipped," the other said. "Left the landlord in the lurch for six months' rent and he's run off!"

"In a hurry, too. Left much behind, although when sold that will not come near to what he owes."

"What my master owes who?" I asked, genuinely confused.

"Why, this building's owner. He who owns this and the next building over."

"P'raps he's over there, then?"

"We tried it. That's shut up as a tomb. And you may not remain here another minute, either. This house, this entire premises is under formal eviction!" the first bailiff shouted.

He pulled me out the chamber door, and I cringed, servant like, and begged. "Is he not upstairs, then? Master?"

"I just told you he isn't."

"He's done a skip, lad. A skip. If you are owed wages…"

"A half-sovereign. I was due a half-sovereign!" I mewled as I let them push me down the stairs to the entry, Thom's clothing upon me.

"No half-sovereign you shall see, my lad, I fear," the constable said to me, more kind then the others. "Here then! Here's a two-penny! Get you some grub."

I looked at the coin in my hand but quickly closed it, as it was so clean and manicured a hand. Certainly not the hand of a servant.

"Now, get you gone!" The stoutest of the two pulled me away from the outside door while the other reached into a leather case he'd left down at the door. He began nailing it shut with hammer and brads, as the other tacked up a printed notice that read: *Eviction of Premises. Do Not Enter!*

I remained at the foot of the outside front steps looking upon all this activity with the greatest of concern.

One of the stout men stepped into the street and whistled. Almost instantly, a coach appeared from around the corner where it must have been waiting and drew up to him. The three officials clambered in.

"Where shall I go?" I pleaded.

"To blazes! You and your damned master!"

"I was due a half-sovereign wages! A half-sovereign!"

But the coach thundered off down the street, swaying from side to side due to the bulk of the two fat men inside.

Only once they had gone did I stop to think. That bitch Vanessa. *She* was the one who'd done a skip and left me holding the bag for six months' rent. No doubt she had taken my money with her, too!

❖

Thom Cullen was able to climb up to the roof of the shop and retrieve his own clothing where I had dropped it, and for which he was grateful.

"Just as you said," I let him know. "We are evicted."

"My messenger friend come by just moments past and I told him so already. He said he knows of chambers for rent. Not fine like these, of course, with cook and butler." He named a street farther south and east, toward the city. And said what the amount was.

"I can pay you but two weeks' wages," I told him. "But I believe I can find you gainful employment through a friend of old. In Lambeth."

I expected Thom to protest, but all he said was, "'Twould be a shame to leave your employ. But I do know that the Metropolitan Transit Line for two cents' fare will bring us both to the chambers I mentioned, and then we can change to an omnibus on south to Lambeth 'cross the bridge."

"You mean that wooden car that runs on rails in a ditch in the ground?" I asked. "You've been in it?"

"Oh yes, sir. It's very handy-like how it goes across the city."

And when I looked sceptical at those words, he added, "It does rattle a bit and sometimes the young ladies all get in a bother when it goes into a tunnel. But it's perfectly safe."

"What kind of bother?"

"Little shrieks and cries. I pay no attention. 'Tis the wave of the future. I seen plans at the one terminus for it to be all underground in seven years' time."

We found a more private spot and rearranged all our clothing in our luggage, the news seller sold us the Transit Line tickets, and soon we were on our way. The rooms, half a street off Tottenham Court Road, were acceptable and I paid for a week in advance. An hour later, Michael Aloysius was surprised to see me but listened carefully to my tale of woe.

"I'm not the problem, Michael," I told him. "I feel responsible for this lad, who I have taken on. If you could find him work."

"That is easy enough. I need a lad here." The wages were half what Thom had been earning, but he was satisfied with the work once it was explained to him, it being "Not hard. A species of clerkship, merely, if more so than previous."

Surprisingly, Michael Aloysius offered to return all that money I'd given him before, when I'd left Tiger Juke's house, assuring me he neither required it, nor since the shop was faring well, had he any need for it to be paid back as a loan. Even so, I promised to return it as I took the welcome money.

With that on hand and my expenses cut so drastically, I still found myself shocked by how easily I'd been taken in and defrauded at the hands of what Thom called "gentlefolk."

It was the younger man who suggested that I go to visit Ex-Queue.

"To what end?"

"Sure, sir, to let him know about it all. He is a close friend. Why don't I go by and drop a card upon his entry table for you? I can do it on my way to return to that shop in Lambeth."

Depressed as I was, I consented, and crossed out my old address and wrote in the new one by hand. Not two hours later, I received Pell's own messenger with a note: *Meet me at the club, at half eight of the clock. We'll dine there. Much of note has occurred.*

Thom Cullen insisted I must be dressed as well as possible for that meeting. "If he is to feed you also, sir," he expostulated. I had to agree. What counted in the world of the clubs was as much *how* you showed your situation as what that situation actually was.

I was expected from previous parties, I was known to the staff, and so shown in, and then into a smaller club chamber, a reading room it appeared, that I was unfamiliar with, furnished by heavy chairs and small tables in between a profusion of tall plants.

I ordered a brandy and soda and wondered how to begin.

I needn't have worried how. The author arrived, his own drink following him into the room by half a minute, and once seated, Pell said all in a rush, "They've done a skip on us. On the club. On everyone."

"Eugene, you mean."

"Damn Eugene! Yes. But more crucially, Tay has done a skip with her. Owing the Lord only knows how much to how many people in the club, of the club, and outside the club. I myself am only in the hole for a loan of twenty pounds, but others..."

I burst into laughter. "Me too. They robbed me blind and left me to face two fat bailiffs and a constable."

"Oh, no!" Pell was equally jocular. "But that's serious for you, lad. You have little means or resources."

"Don't I know it."

Pell stopped a moment. "I see. So, that's why your address was so suddenly changed. But how did you get rid of them bailiffs?"

"I pretended I was my boy, Cullen." We laughed again. "I moaned and complained I was owed half a sovereign."

"More like a hundred sovereigns."

"If not more." And after we had calmed down, I said. "So, Ex, I am to be your dinner guest tonight?"

"Naturally."

Pell had more to say about Vanessa and Lord Tay, but when we finished our drinks over that and were about to get up to head to the dining club room, from behind us I heard a voice suddenly ask, "And so I assume, young man, that you are currently in search of gainful employment?"

Startled, we both stood up. Through the fronds of a Boston fern, I saw a handsome man with a rather flat cap of golden hair, about middle age, of medium girth, and completely "tricked out," as Pell put it, for the club.

Pell recognized him. "My Lord. Sir." Turning to me, he said, "Lord Roland, Earl of R——, this fellow down on his luck for the moment is young Addison Grimmins."

"I believe I have heard that name before," the Earl said.

Still in high spirits, I allowed, "In this club, you well might have."

"And the reports I've received for once do not exaggerate or deceive." Lord Roland held my hand longer. "But I repeat my question. I assume you are in search of gainful employment."

"Kind as the offer is sure to be, Lord Roland, I doubt if our young friend need worry for a living since—"

"You assume correctly, Milord," I interrupted. "I *am* in search of gainful employment. Since, Mr. Pell, you ought to also know that I have formally left my previous lines of employment." Not that I wouldn't return to one, temporarily, I knew, if Lord Roland wanted me to.

But I felt certain somehow that all those previous employments were in truth now in the past and another, more substantial employment to my talents was in the offing.

"I am glad to hear of it," Lord Roland said.

A waiter stepped into the room and requested Pell's attention. Once he was gone, I said, "May I ask what kind of employment, sir?"

"I'll be frank with you. I am in need of a man who can be almost myself."

"That sounds like an impossible role to fill."

"Perhaps not. I need a man who can do *almost* what I can do, but who can go to places and do things where I couldn't *possibly* be, or possibly *be seen*. He must combine elegance, eloquence, and, of course, extreme effectiveness. Does that seem as tall an order?"

"Even taller."

"But not impossible?"

"Not impossible with some coaching, Milord. I am a quick study."

"Don't worry, young sir. You will receive more coaching than you ever thought possible, and in areas you never knew existed before. Enough so that in a few years you will be someone who can do almost what I can do."

I didn't know how to respond to that, and rather sputtered, ending with, "At any rate, one could only do one's best."

Lord Roland pulled a card case out of a breast pocket and quickly wrote something on a card, then handed it to me.

"Shall you come visit my offices at Whitehall tomorrow? In the late morning?"

Pell returned from his confab and Lord Roland added to me, "Please hand this card to whoever tries to bar your entry."

There were half bows all around. The Earl left the club room, leaving me amused and Pell almost with his mouth hanging open.

"Thom Cullen was right to stick by me. He it was who sent me here tonight," I told Pell. "That man very much wishes to hire me."

"Addison, that man who wishes to hire you is one of the three most powerful in the British Empire."

"You don't say."

"I do say. Addison, your fortune is made."

4. Epilogue

To: The Earl of R——
11 Hanover Square
London, England

17 January 188—

Sir,

After the terrible assault by one Mr. MacIlhenny who publicised himself as under your direct orders and who perished in the mêlée, I was told that Addison's very last words before losing consciousness here in Florence referred to some writings of his. Since I am his only living relation, these were easily enough obtained and read here. A fair copy has been sent off to you, along with a packet of letters, exact copies of those Her Ladyship has sent to her new daughter-in-law to be read by her during her honeymoon, lest that young person be "so completely hoodwinked" as the Lady claims to have been after her own nuptials. These have been copied out in my own hand for the purpose of possible prosecution. Her Ladyship said but two sentences: "Your dear Addison is another victim of my far-reaching and vicious husband. I fear that his fate is my fault."

"Had he not interfered," I assured her, "we both would have perished, it is now certain enough to me, as our own little Henriette perished before us." So, I absolve her. Although she was correct ascribing all the blame.

I do not know how you plan to pay for this, Sir, but you have two years to think of it before I return to England to claim my estate, and we shall see then what I may be able to achieve through those with whom I hold great influence.

> Her Ladyship asked myself and the Venetian lad, too, to stay on awhile in her service and to live with her and Mr. Partlett here in Italy, as much for our own comfort as for all our safety. For who knows, she asked, if there is not another assassin sent out in case of failure?
> None of us would be at all surprised.
> Stephen Walter Undershot

❖

"There it is! What do you think?"

"You clearly weren't intending upon being friendly."

"Clearly."

"I think it a fine piece of bravado, threat, misinformation, and persiflage," the Marchioness declared. "Send it off by Ennio. He goes into the village tomorrow, and the mail is picked up to go to Fiesole later that day."

"And you? Brother Addison, what think you of the letter?"

"Exactly as Her Ladyship said," Addison replied. "Do you think he'll ever ask to see an accounting of the monies I secured at various banks and offices for my European jaunt? After all, he *is* the Exchequer."

"*Was* the Exchequer," she said with a little smile. "What he is now is a man with no office, and if my son's latest correspondence is at all correct, he is furthermore someone who is awaiting prosecution for murder."

"But still my brother warns him in any action against himself or yourself."

"Wouldn't you?" Davey asked.

"I suppose."

"Shall you attempt to sit upon that ancient jade of a nag tomorrow as you promised?" she then asked Addison.

"You mean to show how well I have recovered?"

It was already winter. Christmas had come and gone and then the local Italian *Natale*, and they could still sit outside for several hours a day with only light jackets or heavy sweaters, although he was always swaddled like a sour-faced Christ child in one of those ominous-looking village manger scenes.

"We don't care if you do nothing but sit there or lie there and look wonderful," she said decisively. "I rather like the idea that he ended up paying for your grand tour of the Continent."

"It wasn't always terribly grand," Addison said. "But it served its purpose. I am a finished product now. Polished to a fine degree, don't you think? Wasn't that as a rule the purpose of such a tour?"

"It was and you are, albeit with still a few lovely, rough edges."

They heard noise and shouting coming up the pathway into the winter garden. It was Ennio and Luca and some of the smaller daughters of Mr. Partlett's servants here. They all ended up in a comfortable heap at the feet of the British trio.

"Luca wants me to go back to Venice and live with the Comtesse. He's become so spoiled by that, it's all he thinks of."

"Ah, no!" Luca declared, having understood it all. "No spoiled. Happy now. This place."

Addison looked about himself, his brother healthy and comfortable, the lady safe and comfortable, Her beau, Mr. Partlett, with *La Nonna* coming out of the house with little crudités for them to take bits of and a bottle of wine and glasses for them to sip before the sun set and it was time for supper.

Luca was right. Happy now. This place.

About the Author

Felice Picano (http://www.felicepicano.net) is the author of thirty-five books of poetry, fiction, memoirs, and nonfiction. His work is translated into seventeen languages; several titles were national and international bestsellers, including *The Lure*, *Like People in History*, and *The Book of Lies*.

Four of Picano's plays have been produced. He's considered a founder of modern gay literature along with other members of the Violet Quill. He's won or been nominated for numerous awards including being a finalist for five Lammies, and he received the Lambda Literary Foundation's Pioneer Award. A teacher, lecturer, and facilitator of writing workshops, Picano's most recent work is *Justify My Sins: A Hollywood Novel in Three Acts* (2019), *Songs & Poems* (2020), *City on a Star: One—Dryland's End* (2021), and *City on a Star: Two—The Betrothal at Usk* (2021).

Books Available From Bold Strokes Books

Best of the Wrong Reasons by Sander Santiago. For Fin Ness and Orion Starr, it takes a funeral to remind them that love is worth living for. (978-1-63555-867-8)

Coming to Life on South High by Lee Patton. Twenty-one-year-old gay virgin Gabe Rafferty's first adult decade unfolds as an unpredictable journey into sex, love, and livelihood. (978-1-63555-906-4)

Death's Prelude by David S. Pederson. In this prequel to the Detective Heath Barrington Mystery series, Heath discovers that first love changes you forever and drives you to become the person you're destined to be. (978-1-63555-786-2)

His Brother's Viscount by Stephanie Lake. Hector Somerville wants to rekindle his illicit love affair with Viscount Wentworth, but he must overcome one problem: Wentworth still loves Hector's brother. (978-1-63555-805-0)

The Dubious Gift of Dragon Blood by J. Marshall Freeman. One day Crispin is a lonely high school student—the next he is fighting a war in a land ruled by dragons, his otherworldly boyfriend at his side. (978-1-63555-725-1)

Quake City by St John Karp. Can Andre find his best friend Amy before the night devolves into a nightmare of broken hearts, malevolent drag queens, and spontaneous human combustion? Or has it always happened this way, every night, at Aunty Bob's Quake City Club? (978-1-63555-723-7)

Death Overdue by David S. Pederson. Did Heath turn to murder in an alcohol-induced haze to solve the problem of his blackmailer, or was it someone else who brought about a death overdue? (978-1-63555-711-4)

Every Summer Day by Lee Patton. Meant to celebrate every summer day, Luke's journal instead chronicles a love affair as fast-moving and possibly as fatal as his brother's brain tumor. (978-1-63555-706-0)

Everyday People by Louis Barr. When film star Diana Danning hires private eye Clint Steele to find her son, Clint turns to his former West Point barracks mate, and ex-buddy with benefits, Mars Hauser to lend his cyber espionage and digital black ops skills to the case.(978-1-63555-698-8)

Cirque des Freaks and Other Tales of Horror by Julian Lopez. Explore the pleasure of horror in this compilation that delivers like the horror classics…good ole tales of terror. (978-1-63555-689-6)

Royal Street Reveillon by Greg Herren. In this Scotty Bradley mystery, someone is killing the stars of a reality show, and it's up to Scotty Bradley and the boys to find out who. (978-1-63555-545-5)

Death Takes a Bow by David S. Pederson. Alan Keys takes part in a local stage production, but when the leading man is murdered, his partner Detective Heath Barrington is thrust into the limelight to find the killer. (978-1-63555-472-4)

Accidental Prophet by Bud Gundy. Days after his grandmother dies, Drew Morten learns his true identity and finds himself racing against time to save civilization from the apocalypse. (978-1-63555-452-6)

In Case You Forgot by Fredrick Smith and Chaz Lamar. Zaire and Kenny, two newly single, Black, queer, and socially aware men, start again—in love, career, and life—in the West Hollywood neighborhood of LA. (978-1-63555-493-9)

Counting for Thunder by Phillip Irwin Cooper. A struggling actor returns to the Deep South to manage a family crisis but finds love and ultimately his own voice as his mother is regaining hers for possibly the last time. (978-1-63555-450-2)

Survivor's Guilt and Other Stories by Greg Herren. Award-winning author Greg Herren's short stories are finally pulled together into a single collection, including the Macavity Award–nominated title story and the first-ever Chanse MacLeod short story. (978-1-63555-413-7)

Of Echoes Born by 'Nathan Burgoine. A collection of queer fantasy short stories set in Canada from Lambda Literary Award finalist 'Nathan Burgoine. (978-1-63555-096-2)

BOLDSTROKESBOOKS.COM

Looking for your next great read?

Visit BOLDSTROKESBOOKS.COM
to browse our entire catalog of paperbacks, ebooks,
and audiobooks.

Want the first word on what's new?
Visit our website for event info,
author interviews, and blogs.

Subscribe to our free newsletter for sneak peeks,
new releases, plus first notice of promos
and daily bargains.

SIGN UP AT
BOLDSTROKESBOOKS.COM/signup

Bold Strokes Books
Quality and Diversity in LGBTQ Literature

Bold Strokes Books is an award-winning publisher
committed to quality and diversity in LGBTQ fiction.